Kenneth Steven is a poet, children's author and translator. He travels all over the country to give readings and to visit schools to talk about his work. When at home in Perthshire he enjoys walking in the woods and hills that surround the village where he lives with his wife Ute.

February
the
29th

KENNETH STEVEN

For Jessica,
All best wishes,

Kenn R Steve

ARGYLL✠PUBLISHING

© Kenneth Steven 2009

Argyll Publishing
Glendaruel
Argyll PA22 3AE
Scotland
www.argyllpublishing.com

www.kennethsteven.co.uk
e-mail:info@kennethsteven.co.uk

The author has asserted
his moral rights.

British Library Cataloguing-in-Publication Data.
A catalogue record for this book is available from the British Library.

ISBN 978 1 906134 31 0

Cover Art & Illustrations
Louise Ho

Printing
Athenaeum Press, Gateshead

This book is for Moray,
without whom uncle Nichol
would never have been.

•

'Toby? Toby! Are you awake?'

It was his dad and he knew at once that it was very early in the morning. He opened his eyes and struggled round in the darkness. His dad was sitting at the bottom of the bed.

'Listen, old fellow, I'm sorry to waken you so early. It's been quite a night. I had to take your mum back into hospital at two in the morning and it's about seven now. It's all right, I've been on the phone to the ward and she's doing fine, but they'll keep her in for the time being.'

Toby rubbed the sleep from his eyes and put on the bedside light.

'The thing is, Toby, we're going to have to move from here. Yes, I know how much you love the house but it's just not right for us now. Your mum can't manage these stairs, Toby. Imagine if she were to fall? So I'm going to have to do some searching. Somewhere closer to the hospital. I'll do my best to find somewhere that feels like home, I promise. But that means I'm going to be on the hoof for the next few days, I'm afraid. No, you can't come with me, Toby, that just wouldn't work. I know it's your birthday, we both know it's your birthday, but this wasn't something we ever imagined happening. You have to make the best of it, old fellow. Now listen, I've spoken to uncle Nichol, and he's more than happy for you to be out with him at Alumbria until I'm back and we know what we're doing. Please, Toby, you have to try to see we're all doing the best we can. . . '

1. Getting There

The train was very slow. Toby sighed and looked out of the window as they squealed to a halt for the four hundred and seventy-fifth time.

'Would you like another mint, dear?'

The old lady across the carriage from him was holding out the same paper bag of sweets. She had one tucked in her cheek, making her look as if she had a gum boil.

'No, thank you, I'm fine.'

He managed a smile. An hour it had taken them from Edinburgh and still they had maybe another hour to go. Already it was almost dark and it was only four o'clock. It was February and everything was wet. The grey branches dripped grey water and the grey railway tracks disappeared into grey mist. Trust him to have a birthday in February. And now he was going to his mad uncle Nichol's.

But that made him remember his mum. The last time he'd seen her was in hospital, propped up against three big white pillows. Her cheeks were all pink but he knew that wasn't because she was well. Toby had tried to be cheery for her sake, but he felt as if he was swimming through very deep water when he went to sit down at the bottom of her bed. All he wanted in the world was to bury his head in her hair and cry. Her hair always smelled so sweet and gold, like hay. But the only smell that was there was the hospital antiseptic and it made him feel sick. And he was there because his mum had cancer, and he didn't know if she would get better.

That was yesterday. The day he'd been told he was going for a fortnight to his uncle Nichol's. His first thought was that he wouldn't see his mum on his birthday. Then he wondered if that was selfish. No, more than anything else he wanted to be with his mum on his birthday. He cried because he was angry and he cried because he didn't want to go to uncle Nichol's.

His uncle Nichol lived in a big wooden house called Alumbria in the middle of a field. He had a horse, at least three goats, and two St Bernards. He had a great mop of grey hair that he never combed and he was forever inventing things. Except that nothing ever really lasted. He just seemed to recycle what didn't work and start on something new. Uncle Nichol was likely to have breakfast in the middle of the night and dinner in the bath.

The train lurched into motion. At this rate he wouldn't get to Alumbria till midnight. He shivered. Maybe he'd have to walk the last of the way on his own, down the old farm track. Of course he'd forgotten to bring a torch with him.

The train grew faster and the evening darker. Far away Toby could see a town, its lights glinting and winking. He felt so lonely, lonelier than ever before in his life. The only good thing was that he was missing school for two whole weeks. At least Billy Cartwright wouldn't have the joy of shouting 'Only three today! It's Toby Goodwin's third birthday, boys!' But not even that made him feel very happy.

Toby Goodwin had been born in a rather ordinary hospital on a rather ordinary Friday night. Well, except that the date on the calendar had been February the 29th, for it had been a leap year. That was why Billy Cartwright would have had a great deal of pleasure in mocking him, because theoretically he'd only celebrated two *real* birthdays since he was born. This was going to be the third one, this February, and he was going to spend it at uncle Nichol's.

'You and I are special, boy,' uncle Nichol had once said to him, placing a heavy hand on his head. Toby had looked up at him with large eyes, waiting for an explanation. 'You were born on February the 29th and I've been struck by lightning twice.'

'Is that why you have such funny hair?' Toby had asked, looking up at the grey tufts sticking straight into the air.

Uncle Nichol had taken away his hand. 'As a matter of fact you're absolutely right,' he'd replied astonished. 'I'd never thought of it before but you're absolutely right. But there were far bigger things it did to me,' he had said darkly, and walked away to put another log on the fire.

The train was really speeding now. Toby found a scrap of paper and worked out just how far they had to go. It was a difficult sum, but he didn't mind that. He loved maths more than anything else in the world, and nobody else in his family could understand it.

'Toby would do sums at Christmas Dinner,' his mother once said when the some friends came round one evening. He had smiled shyly but didn't argue with her – it was probably true. If he felt down or worried nothing cheered him up as much as arithmetic. Figures didn't have feelings, they didn't change according to their thoughts. They were reliable. They were always there.

He worked out they had forty-six minutes to go. All of a

sudden he realised he didn't want to get off the train. It was warm and snug and the dark outside was uninviting. And soon he would be on his way to Alumbria. . .

But forty-six minutes later they were there. Toby dragged off two cases and a large rucksack and the little old lady who'd sat opposite him waved as the train pulled out of the station once more. It was like a glowing, yellow caterpillar.

'Excuse me, young sir. Would you happen to be Daniel Goodwin?' The station manager was looking at him intently in the darkness. Toby nodded wearily. Uncle Nichol always called him Daniel – had done since his first 'real' birthday.

'Your uncle says he's afraid you'll have to walk. The car battery went flat on Tuesday and he hasn't been into town.'

That was uncle Nichol all right. Probably he'd been too busy building an aeroplane powered by cheese or some strange kind of windmill to operate the electricity. Toby said good night, heaved the rucksack onto his shoulders, and started off down the lane. It wasn't actually all that far, he told himself. Maybe a quarter of a mile. He glanced up at the skies. There was a good bit of moon there – the trouble was that a lot of the time it was behind clouds.

The dark was much darker than you realised all the same. Once the station with its lights had been left behind there was nothing, just the cold rustling of the wind and the trees shifting like strange, mocking watchers. They were all watching him. He stopped to straighten the rucksack and swap hands with the cases. He looked about him, feeling that horrible sense that something was there at his back, breathing down his neck. The trouble was, he couldn't run, not even if he'd wanted to.

2. Alumbria

At last Toby caught sight of the lights of Alumbria. The big house was shining like a Christmas tree, and up in the attics the brightness seemed particularly strong. He wasn't looking forward to this, but at least it was good to know he was safe, and the cases felt as if they were filled with rocks.

He found the front door wide open. A sleek black cat that seemed the size of a young puma was staring at him with golden slits of eyes. Someone was running about upstairs singing 'Land of Hope and Glory'. (It was said that uncle Nichol had once been married but that his wife had stormed out one winter night, taking nothing but the hoover with her. It was said she couldn't stand the untidiness a moment longer).

Toby put down the case in his left hand and knocked.

'Hello,' he said gingerly. 'Hello.'

There was a fearful thump upstairs followed by a long string of very bad words.

'Daniel? Is that you, Daniel?' A white face appeared at an angle round the edge of the banister two floors up. Looking up that high made Toby feel a little seasick. He hadn't answered before there was a thundering of feet and with a great flourish his uncle was there in the hallway.

'My dear boy! I'm so sorry about the car! You see I'm doing something very important.' He gestured towards the cat. 'You

11

remember Malice? Dear Malice wouldn't hurt a fly, well certainly not someone of your size. A good journey? Have you eaten?'

He bustled and chattered so much Toby's head felt like a washing machine.

Toby still hadn't stepped over the threshold. But it wasn't long before he was enjoying a cup of very black tea, some hot buttered toast, and as much almond cake as he could eat.

'You know about mum?' Toby asked in a soft voice, when at last there was a gap in the conversation. Malice leapt up onto her master's lap and he scratched her ears. She could have purred for England.

Uncle Nichol nodded very slowly and closed his eyes as he did so.

'Oh yes, Daniel, I do. I do indeed. But don't you despair. Don't you despair, I tell you.'

All of a sudden Toby felt terribly tired. He looked at the great grandfather clock in the corner of the sitting room and saw that it was almost midnight.

'You get up whenever you want in the morning,' his uncle told him as if he could read his thoughts. 'I've a whole lot to do and in the afternoon I need to get that blasted car fixed. If you want a bath, there's enough hot water to. . .' He stopped as if stuck for words. 'Well for at least the whole of Greenland.' He leaned forward. 'You know how, Daniel?' His eyes were glinting like emeralds.

Toby shook his head but he was sure he was going to find out anyway.

'Geo-thermals!' his uncle hissed.

Toby hadn't the foggiest what geo-thermals were.

'I dug and dug till I hit them,' uncle Nichol said triumph-antly, 'And now I've free hot water for the rest of my life. What pleases me most is that I save on those wretched heating bills and don't have to pay that blasted council. Anyway, you remember where the bath is? Help yourself to a towel, and sleep like a felled tree!'

Toby took what he needed from the rucksack and decided to leave the cases where they were in the hall until the morning. The house smelled just as he remembered it – a mixture of old leather, apples, soot, dust, carpets and dead flies. It made him want to sneeze.

Little faces peered out at him from old chairs on the landing, and sometimes he nearly jumped with fright as he caught sight of his own reflection in little round mirrors. There were books that looked as though they hadn't been touched for forty years, with pictures of strange countries and titles he couldn't read.

His room was freezing cold. A tiny branch from one of the trees outside was tapping against the window like an old finger. Toby switched on the lamp and saw his huge shadow reflected on the far wall. He shivered. He would have that bath in the morning. Five minutes later he was asleep.

3. The Mystery Begins

When Toby woke up next morning the wind had dropped and sunlight was pouring into his bedroom. There wasn't a sound to be heard so he knew that uncle Nichol had gone, that the house was empty. He felt more like himself, but he thought at once of his mother in hospital and wondered how she was. He wouldn't have had the first idea where his uncle kept the telephone – for all he knew it might be in the kitchen sink.

He wandered up a little staircase to the bathroom. It was in the strangest sort of turret you could imagine – sticking up from the side of the house, the steps and the panels all made of wood. At the top it opened up into a round room that was surrounded on three sides by lattice windows. That morning it was like coming into a blue pool, for the skies outside were completely clear and the sun was streaming in from the east. A flock of pigeons rose from the roof of the house and scattered in soft shadows.

Toby ran the hot tap. He remembered what his uncle had said about the water coming straight up from the ground. It bubbled and spat as it came through, and there was enough steam from it for half a dozen dragons. It was a strange blue colour, looking almost like liquid sky. It took a long time to cool it to the right temperature, but eventually it felt just right and he slid in and lay there, looking up at the sunlight. His uncle had made a balsa wood mobile that hung from the ceiling; it was a kind of circus wheel with four cyclists. The heat of the water underneath spun them round; the hotter the water, the faster the cyclists circled.

What was particularly nice about the bath was that Toby could lie completely flat in it. The worst of the one at home was that it was far too short. He always had his knees sticking up out of the water, so part of him ended up far too hot and the rest of him miles too cold. And in Edinburgh the whole bathroom shook with the rattle of lorries and traffic. That made him think about his dad and his search for a new house. He wondered where he was and what he would find.

Suddenly he felt a lot better about being at uncle Nichol's. He had dreaded coming, and there were still plenty of things he disliked, but on the whole he was a lot happier than he had been. The last weeks had been awful, going as often as possible to the hospital and still trying to concentrate on homework. His dad had done his best to cheer him, but neither of them had felt very happy. There was no use pretending. Everything felt strange – it wasn't like home.

It had snowed one night, and by the morning the streets were just brown and mushy and the skies all dirty and dark. He felt more unhappy than ever before in his whole life, and at night he did sums in bed to comfort himself. As he heard the planes circling over the city he sat up working out all sorts of strange sums, as if somehow it would help to solve them even when he couldn't solve so much else.

He was only a couple of hours away from Edinburgh and yet somehow it felt an awful lot further. Perhaps it was because they were right out in the middle of the countryside – there wasn't a busy road rushing with cars nearby; there were no jumbo jets over the house roof in the middle of the night. There was just one very mad uncle and his very strange cat.

He turned round as if he knew someone was there and looked right into the round eyes of Malice. She was glaring over at him from the bathroom door that he'd forgotten to close. Toby guessed that maybe this was her hideout, that he was intruding.

He didn't want to leave his deliciously warm wallow, but in the end his fingers and toes became all wrinkly and he came out.

'Now you can have the place to yourself, Malice,' he said. Malice just hissed as he passed her on the stairs.

He went down, thinking that a bit of breakfast would be a very good idea. He reckoned it must be about ten o'clock. The kitchen looked as if it had last been dusted sometime just before the Russian Revolution. Everything was where it shouldn't be and nothing was where it should have been. He found shoes where he expected to find pans, candles where he was hoping for cutlery and a dragonfly in a box in the fridge. Then he found a note on the kitchen table, in among keys and carrots and piles of weird-looking drawings.

Welcome to Alumbria! Enjoy the house and enjoy the garden – but whatever you do, don't go up to the attic.
See you after lunch.   *Uncle Nichol*

He frowned. What was the secret in the attic he wasn't to see? A birthday present, perhaps?

The question tickled him. So, of course, the attic was one of the places he'd most love to go. Still, he tried to put the thought out of his head. He finally managed to find some bread, so healthy and brown he could barely chew it, and a teabag.

For a second he looked round automatically for the television, since in Edinburgh it was almost always on. But there was no television in this house. That was what made Alumbria so strange – it was a bit like an island in the middle of nowhere. It existed quite apart from the world outside, and somehow normal time didn't function there. It had its own time, was half an hour behind everywhere else. You began to forget about the rest of the world here – it was its own little world.

When he was done he went outside. He was half-blinded by the sun that came streaming down across the fields in a great golden splash, as if a big bucket of sunlight had been dropped out of the clouds. Then he was toppled over by two dogs the size of small horses and didn't know quite where he was for a moment. Tweedledum and Tweedledee were uncle Nichol's two St Bernards, and although they were quite enormous they were as soft as butter and would have been more than content to lick Toby to death.

He got up again having had his second wash of the morning! The dogs came with him to see the three goats who were in their shelter munching. Uncle Nichol called them the Three Wise Men, and Toby thought they did look rather wise. Their great gold eyes shone like giant marbles and their beards trailed down over their chests.

'So what's the square root of forty-nine, then?' Toby

whispered. The three goats stared at him, chewing all the time.

'I see, so it's too easy for you,' Toby said. 'You're not bothering to answer.'

All at once with a stab he thought of what his uncle had written about the attic. What was it he was hiding? He wished he could go up there. He couldn't wait to know the surprise. As he came out again onto the grass he found himself half-turning; his uncle wouldn't be home for another hour or two. If he went up now he'd have more than enough time. . .

But he couldn't. At the last minute he stopped himself, not wanting uncle Nichol to be angry with him. He'd never seen uncle Nichol angry, but he wasn't sure he wanted to. He'd go and see the library instead. Reluctantly he turned away from the house.

The library was uncle Nichol's special den. He built it after once having a strange dream, and it was Toby's favourite place at Alumbria.

'I saw a black knight on a charger, Daniel. He was riding up to a little tower, in the middle of a wood, and suddenly I knew this was his very own secret place. Magical. And it was full of books.'

His uncle's eyes had sparkled in the firelight as he told Toby about the dream.

The boy went into the tight circle of pine trees and fought his way through to a mossy clearing. The amazing thing was that you would never have known the little tower was there at all – from the garden it just looked as if there was a very deep pine wood.

The tower was like a pencil, with a spiky top. It was made

of bright, sparkling stone that his uncle had told him was called granite. There were little slits of windows here and there in the circular wall and a low wooden door that Toby opened to go inside.

The first thing you saw as you came in was the chimney – a shiny, metal pipe that disappeared up through the whole tower. When the fire was lit at the bottom the metal pipe became beautifully hot and the tower could be cosy on the wildest of winter nights.

As Toby's eyes grew used to the dark he saw the narrow wooden staircase that curled up from the ground floor. Down here uncle Nichol kept all sorts of useless things – boxes of Christmas lights, watches that no longer told the time, shoes he'd long since grown out of, and bundles and bundles of papers. Toby stepped through the mess and started up the staircase, having left the little wooden door open behind him. He climbed to the upper floor. All that was there round the walls were books, on astronomy, fishing, history, poetry, weaving, languages and art, and a hundred other subjects besides. Toby loved the smell of the old books in particular; he sniffed their leather covers and always wanted to sneeze.

But the staircase didn't stop there. It curled on up into a last tiny chamber, only high enough to crouch in, with a soft round bed. Toby looked up at it and suddenly thought of his uncle and the note. A hot rush of excitement filled his head and made him dizzy. He could pretend he'd never even found the note in the first place!

Why was his uncle so keen for him not to go up to the attic? The thought bothered him, buzzed about in his head like a bluebottle. Any other time he'd have loved nothing more than to stay where he was in the tower and read, all snug up on the floor of the library. But he knew it would be useless. He couldn't get the question out of his mind now that it was there.

He went back down and closed the tower door behind him. He found the dogs again when he broke back through the trees. They scampered about, wanting him to play, but somehow he didn't have the heart to begin throwing sticks for them and chasing all over the garden.

He would have a very, very quick look – nothing more than that. He got in just in time to hear the last ring of a telephone – Toby stood in the hall and listened to its echo fading away. At once he thought of his mother. He saw her in his mind's eye in all that whiteness, with the strange and terrible machines blinking around her. She had looked so small. He had wanted more than anything else in the world to rescue her but he just hadn't know how. . . His eyes burned hot and angry. He forced himself not to think like this because it was useless. It solved nothing.

The sun poured into the hall in a long pillar of gold and Malice flopped down in the middle of it, staring up at Toby with malevolent eyes.

'So what's uncle Nichol hiding from us in the attic?' Toby breathed, daring to scratch Malice's ears.

The cat growled, and bounded away upstairs, as if leading the way to the attic. Toby turned for a last time towards the front door, holding his breath, and then started up the stairs himself, taking them two at a time.

The upper house was a bit spooky, even amid the brightness of that late February morning. Uncle Nichol probably

hadn't cleaned there for about twenty-six and a half years, and the corridors and stairs were cluttered with weird African masks, musical instruments made of dark wood, and broken pottery. There was a smell there that was somehow green and bad. . . Once when Toby was just seven, his uncle had asked him to go up there to find a certain book. It had been a windy November evening and the stairs creaked. When Toby bent to pick up the book his uncle wanted, something slid from a railing and he had chased back downstairs, terrified out of his wits. His uncle, his white hair wilder than ever, had laughed until the tears ran down his cheeks. But Toby had refused to go back up those stairs on his own. . .

Something of that fear crept back into him now. Malice brushed against his legs and he almost shrieked. One look and he'd go downstairs again anyway, that was what he'd decided. He switched on the last light and looked up into the high rafters. There was a kind of booming from them, as if they were loose. There was something shining up there under the ceiling, but the light was so bad it was impossible to tell what it was. He peered and he squinted, but from where he was standing he couldn't quite tell. It was like some kind of cylinder.

He just had time to glance down at his feet and see a folder with <u>February the 29th</u> written at the top, when he heard a distant thud below him.

'Daniel? That's me back. Where are you?'

Toby's mouth went dry. He closed his eyes and wished the floorboards would swallow him up.

4. The Story

He sat in an armchair waiting for his uncle. That was it. He was probably going to be sent back to Edinburgh that very day, the shame of what he'd done ringing in his ears. His uncle had asked him to wait in the study. Malice was sitting on the rug in front of the fire, her eyes full of what Toby was sure was gloating.

'So you went up into the attic?'

His uncle burst into the study, a tray of steaming mugs of hot chocolate in his hands.

'I can't tell you how sorry I am. . .'

'Too late, Daniel.' He put down the tray with a flourish and looked round. The corners of his mouth were twisting. . .

'I knew you'd go up there!' he roared, and his laughter sent Malice over the room in a black streak.

Toby couldn't understand a thing. Wasn't he angry?

'It's the oldest temptation in the world!' his uncle said, flopping down into a chair opposite. 'Adam and Eve and the apple? The greatest temptation is the one thing you can't have! It sticks in your mind, won't go away. And I was right.'

'What is up there, then?' Toby asked, his hands cupped round the mug. 'I saw something. . . '

'I'll tell you this evening,' his uncle said. 'Not before then.'

And he wagged his finger at his nephew as he sipped his hot chocolate.

All the rest of that day Toby waited. He spoke to his mother on the phone and she was glad to hear his voice; he could almost hear her smiling weakly as she spoke and that made him find it difficult to speak. More than anything else in the world he wanted her to be well again. It seemed strange hearing his mum's voice there at Alumbria. There was the phone in a muddle of shoes and books and ornaments, and he was speaking to his mum in the hospital ward where he'd last seen her. She sounded tired – very, very, tired. His dad was still hunting for a house; he hadn't seen anything that felt just right yet.

He sat in his room for a while after that, waiting and thinking. He tried to read a book for a bit but he couldn't concentrate, and when he looked up he saw to his surprise that it was snowing. Tiny silver flakes were spiralling down from the sky. He went over to the window, letting his book fall to the floor.

Already the trees around Alumbria looked as if they had been dusted with sugar. Maybe if there was enough by the following day he'd be able to go sledging. It was so wonderfully still outside, the way it always is when it's snowing. It's somehow more than silence, even quieter than complete quiet. It's the quietest quiet there can be, and Toby stayed at the windowsill a long time, hoping the flakes would become bigger, that they really would settle.

He helped his uncle bring in wood for the fire and cut some sticks for kindling. (Uncle Nichol said that was his punishment for going up to see what was in the attic, though Toby felt that was slightly unfair since his uncle had known he would give in to temptation.) But he didn't say anything, and after that he came in to warm his hands on the fire since they hurt with the cold. It was beginning to get dark and the snow was still twirling out of the skies like tiny ballet dancers. Toby reckoned it couldn't be long before evening had come and he could find out what was in the attic.

But then his uncle had a letter to write and the goats to see to. He had to check on something out in the sheds and was gone for so long that Toby almost despaired of him coming back at all. When finally he did come into the study he was covered in snowflakes from head to foot. He didn't bother to shake them off his jumper and trousers but just slumped down in an armchair and looked at Toby without blinking.

'Did I ever tell you how I came to be struck twice by lightning?' he said softly.

'You were going to tell me about the attic,' his nephew reminded him.

Uncle Nichol waved that thought away like a fly.

'The first time I was just sixteen. Your mother was a bit younger and she was at home, but I went out to camp in the woods. During the night there was a terrible storm – the thunder and lightning were so close together I knew the storm was almost right overhead. I poked my head out of the tent and the lightning struck a rock just ten feet away. It split it right in two – like a knife going through a potato. All the ground round about turned bright silver – and so did my hair. At sixteen I went grey and my hair's never stayed flat on my head since.'

Malice jumped onto his knee and began her black purring.

'Were you made fun of at school?' Toby asked.

His uncle thought about that a bit. It was as if little wheels were going round inside his head. 'Maybe it got a bit worse,' he said in the end. 'But I don't think it made that much difference. If people are going to make fun of you, they'll do it anyway.'

Toby nodded. He knew all about that all right. He could hear Billy Cartwright's laughter somewhere in his head.

'What about the second time then?' he asked, suddenly remembering.

His uncle stretched forward in the chair and look at him intently once more.

'I was sailing to America in a ship called the *Queen Mary*,' he said, his voice quiet, almost as if he was afraid someone else was listening. 'I'd been doing lots of things with my life, but nothing very important or worthwhile. I got bored very easily, and I was always running away to find something I thought would be better. There was one beautiful night we were right out in the middle of the Atlantic Ocean and I'd left the curtains over the porthole open so I could see the sky. The storm just seemed to come out of nowhere. It was some-how magical, impossible. There was a great flickering and all of a sudden there was this ball of light at the bottom of my bed, a ball of lightning. It was the most amazing thing in the world. And somehow I knew there and then that science was the best thing there was. I knew I had to study science. And you know what that lightning gave me, that second time I was struck by it? It gave me courage!'

'And then you came home?' Toby asked. Malice's purring was becoming deafeningly loud.

'Not quite, but not long after. But for ever afterwards I

wanted to know how things worked. I wanted to invent things.'

Toby was amazed at Malice's purring. 'Haven't you ever thought of using that purr in the house?'

His uncle looked at him with his head on one side.

'You mean purr power?' he said. 'I suppose we could just about run your bedside lamp off an hour or two of Malice at full purr. But somebody would need to keep stroking her!'

Toby laughed.

'All right,' his uncle yawned. 'Time's marching on and I made you a promise. Suddenly he scooped up a most disgruntled Malice and put her, yowling, onto the ground. 'But I'm not going to tell you here. I have a surprise for you! Go and get your coat – wrap up as warm as you can.'

Toby didn't need to be told twice.

He wrapped a scarf his mum had knitted for him about eight times round his neck and put on his boots. It was freezing outside. Ice crystals glittered on a deep layer of snow, but the big flakes themselves were no longer falling. And as Toby's eyes grew used to the dark, he saw two familiar shadows standing a little distance away.

'Tweedledum and Tweedledee!' he exclaimed.

The two St Bernards turned round to look at him, but then Toby saw that they had harnesses round their necks and that there was a little sledge behind them.

He looked round incredulous at his uncle.

'First there's something I want to look at,' uncle Nichol said, 'then we'll go over to the library. I'm afraid neither of us will be in bed before midnight.'

The two of them got onto the little sledge. Uncle Nichol crouched at the front, holding the reins, while Toby stood behind him. Everything was pure silver, as if the trees and hills and distant house had been poured out of a mould for metal. And the stars glittered up above, their yellow and sapphire flames crackling in the black skies. The sledge hissed over the soft snow, and Toby could hear the panting of the two dogs. But all of a sudden uncle Nichol stopped the sledge and stood tall, craning his neck as if trying to see something.

Toby wanted to ask what it was, but at the last minute he didn't. His uncle was muttering things to himself, things that sounded like calculations, and Toby wondered what on earth it could be. Suddenly he thought of what he'd seen in the attic earlier that day – the mysterious tall shape and the folder with February the 29th on it. His uncle took out a little note-book from his pocket and scribbled something down. He seemed pleased with the result, whatever it was.

'I'll race you to the library,' he said, half turning round.

'That's not fair,' Toby said. 'You'll always win because you're the one in front!'

But his uncle only laughed.

Suddenly Toby remembered something. It came like a picture into his mind, not clear, but all misty and vague, like in a dream. He could see his mother there beside him, and Uncle Nichol was shouting something as they chased over deep snow. His dad was running beside the sledge, urging the dogs on and laughing.

'We've done this before!' Toby called out. The wind was sharp in his face as the sledge raced back in the direction of the house and the library and he had to hold onto his uncle lest he lose his balance. Tweedledum and Tweedledee were running for all they were worth.

'You're right, Daniel, you're quite right! It was your fourth birthday and you were all here at Alumbria. I think it was the first time you'd ever really seen snow!'

It was coming back to Toby now. His fourth birthday – or his first, depending on how you looked at it. The first time he'd seen snow and the first memory he had of February the 29th, his real birthday. He'd been so excited he'd thought his heart would burst.

Uncle Nichol slowed the sledge down as they neared the trees beside the library.

'You go off in, Daniel, and get the fire lit. There's plenty of wood by the store. I'll take the sledge back and see to the dogs – we can't leave them out here while we're inside. I won't be long.'

Uncle Nichol disappeared into the dark, looking like a very odd Santa Claus. Toby stood there for a minute, gazing up at the stars and listening to the quiet. He felt excited and yet he didn't quite know why. Very, very far away he heard a church bell ringing out ten slow times.

He opened the little door of the library for the second time that day and lit the old oil lamp that uncle Nichol kept on the windowsill. He liked it so much better than normal electric light. Then he opened the stove door and put in some dry pieces of kindling and a few birch logs. The first two matches he lit broke, but the flame of the third was clear and strong. Soon there was crackling and hissing from the twigs and Toby shut the door once more. There was a little glass window in it and Toby could see the orange flames beginning to creep up the sides of the pipe. Already it was growing warmer.

He sat there after that, cross-legged, staring into the flames and thinking of nothing and everything. In two days' time it would be his birthday. He thought again of his mum, and he saw in his mind the flecks of snow drifting past her hospital window as she lay there, not sleeping. Everything round his mum was white – the sheets, the pillows, the walls, the floors, the nurses, the snow. What was she thinking of? He concentrated so hard he really could feel himself sitting there at the end of the bed watching her. . .

The door banged loudly and Toby jumped with surprise. It was uncle Nichol.

'Well done with the fire. Come on upstairs and let's get warm. My hands are so cold I'm surprised they haven't fallen off. . . ' Toby led the way, the lantern held in his right hand so that his uncle could see the way up the spiral staircase to the library. They could hear the roar of the flames as they leapt up the chimney.

'Right, confession time!' his uncle said, fixing him with a glare. 'What did you see in that attic of mine?'

Toby was rather taken aback. Sometimes he didn't know whether his uncle was being serious or not.

'Only a folder really. With February the 29th written across it.'

A smile spread across uncle Nichol's face. It was like watching flame catch hold of a bit of paper; the smile curled the ends of his lips until the middle turned upwards too.

'So you didn't find all of my secret?' he said very quietly.

Toby shook his head emphatically.

Uncle Nichol got up and went over to one of the bookshelves set into the tower wall. Immediately he discovered the book that he was looking for. It looked in the most awful state – little more than a huddle of a few pages held together by gravity and some rather dirty-looking bits of string. Toby was tempted to smile – if this was at the heart of the secret then he wasn't very impressed.

'Do you remember when I went to Egypt two summers ago?' uncle Nichol asked.

Toby frowned. 'I think so. Is that when you nearly got eaten by a crocodile?'

'Yes, and had to barter almost everything I brought with me to pay for a taxi ride to the airport because I was going to miss my flight. Well, this is one of the things I managed to come home with. I found it in Luxor, down one of the back streets where an old man was selling a whole hillside of books. I'd eaten something very bad the day before and my tummy was going round in circles, but I managed to summon up the strength to go through about five hundred books. Until I got to this.'

'And what's that got to do with the attic?' Toby giggled.

'Patience, boy, patience,' uncle Nichol said, and swept back his hair with his hand so it stood on end even more than ever. 'It has a very great deal to do with the attic. This is a Latin text, and it's an original document from the time of the height of the Roman Empire. Fortunately in my day we still had Latin at school, not like you poor brutes who study useless things like fractions and equations.'

Toby rolled his eyes. His uncle had hated maths at school.

'It tells an amazing story, a story you might think is nothing more than a fantasy, about the visit to somewhere called the Little Moon. And this is where the folder you saw in the attic comes in and becomes important, Daniel. How often does February the 29th happen?'

'Once every four years,' Toby said immediately. That was obvious.

His uncle gave him the tiniest of nods. 'And in this text I found out that once every four years, on February the 29th, the Little Moon appears between us and the moon we know, the big moon.'

Toby looked at him a little doubtfully. 'But why is it we don't know about it? Why hasn't it been talked about?'

Uncle Nichol leaned close to him. 'Because I believe the astronomers don't *want* us to know,' he said in a loud whisper.

Toby's first thought was that his uncle was completely and utterly, barking mad. He was daft as a brush, mad as a hatter, off his rocker – a total and complete lunatic. A prickle of sweat tickled his neck. He didn't know what on earth to say.

'The Romans went there, Daniel,' his uncle went on. 'They went there all right. That's what I believe and a lot of this book is about the first journey to the Little Moon.'

Toby wasn't so worried about that. 'But why would they want to cover it up?' he frowned, thinking aloud.

'Who? You mean the astronomers? Oh, Toby, that isn't all that difficult. There are lots of things that are covered up, things that they think are going to be too frightening for us, or that we're not ready for yet. I'll tell you this, I reckon that many of the people who see UFOs have really been seeing the Little Moon.'

'What about the attic then?' Toby asked suspiciously.

His uncle's eyes sparkled like sapphires. 'A rocket!' he breathed.

'For the last six months I've been working on a rocket, a rocket that will reach the Little Moon. On February the 29th.'

Toby thought about what he was hearing. There were strange thoughts working at the back of his head – he was working them out bit by bit. His heart hammered in his chest.

'You've been working away on this rocket while my mother was so ill in hospital!' Toby got to his feet, his heart hammering in his chest. That wasn't all. 'You never came to visit her! You simply don't care! You're only interested in your stupid inventions!'

The tears filled his eyes and he turned away towards the staircase.

'Daniel, please come back! You're right about the hospital, but it isn't because I don't care. I once had to be in there for six months and I've had a horror of hospitals ever since. It's no excuse, but please listen to me, Daniel! You don't understand! I do care!'

But it was too late. He didn't want to hear another word. He had heard enough. He was sobbing now and the tears spilled down his cheeks. He had to find the quiet and safety of his own room. He thudded down the spiral staircase, hardly seeing where to place his feet on the steps. He marched over to the little door, his uncle still pleading from upstairs for him to come back. He went out and banged the door behind him. If he could he'd have started walking to Edinburgh there and then. He hated Alumbria and he hated his uncle. He'd never come back for the rest of his life. It was an awful place, full of mad inventions and a mad inventor. And his uncle didn't care about anybody but himself. He marched off through the snow towards the house, crying bitterly.

5. The Rocket

During the night the wind got up. It blew the snow into little ledges; it turned it into strange waves over the fields and hedges. The moon rose over Scotland and turned everything into beaten silver. You could see for miles that night. You could see the hills of the Highlands and the church spires of Aberdeen. Except that everyone was asleep, there was almost no-one standing at a window watching the great net of the light sweep down and catch everything in its path.

Toby slipped in and out of sleep. In his dreams his uncle was talking to him, but he was speaking a language Toby couldn't understand. His uncle gave him a Latin dictionary and Toby tried to keep up with all he said, leafing from one word to the next. But all the words were to do with science and they didn't make any more sense in English than they had in Latin.

Then he dreamed he was walking all the way to Edinburgh. His feet were cold because he wasn't wearing any shoes, but he knew that he had to get to his mother in time. There was something he had to do. He reached the hospital where she was and when he went inside his bare feet made no sound on the stairs as he climbed, and none of the nurses in the corridors noticed him. He went into his mother's bedroom and he found that her window was wide open. The snow had blown in and he went over to close it. His mother opened her eyes and smiled, and in his dream he knew he had done all he needed to make her well again. He had closed the window so she wouldn't be cold any more. It was that simple. A great wave of relief and happiness poured into his heart and suddenly it wasn't winter any longer; it was springtime. Flowers were growing up through the little ridges of snow – crocuses and snowdrops and primroses.

Then he woke up again and somehow he knew that his uncle was there in the room. Toby didn't turn round because he remembered just in time that he was still mad at him. He knew it was very early in the morning; it wasn't completely dark any more but the light that was in the room was very grey and weak. He lay there listening, only blinking his eyes.

'Toby. Are you awake?'

'No'

He was sure he could hear his uncle smiling. 'Would you like some cocoa?'

'No.'

He heard his uncle shifting where he was sitting on the chair beside the door.

'I had to come and talk to you, Toby, explain things to you.'

Suddenly he realised his uncle was not calling him Daniel. He couldn't ever remember a time he'd used his real name. He didn't turn round but he sat up on one elbow. His head still felt woolly with dreams and he'd have loved to go back to sleep.

'You're a mathematician, Toby, and I'm a scientist. Neither of us is all that good with words. I know that's an excuse but it's true too.' There was a big sigh.

'I know what you think of me, that you believe I've done all this for fun because I'm nothing more that a mad inventor. Well, maybe you're right, Toby, but I don't think so. That book I told you I found, the one I picked up in Luxor. It told me something else, something I can't tell you about yet. I'm frightened I might be wrong, frightened I might be hoping too much and making you hope too much too. But all I can tell you is that I did build this rocket for your mother. I may not show it but I love her very much. My way is to do things, not say them. And I needed you too, Toby. I needed you to come and help me, that's true. I needed your mathematics.'

Toby turned round, very slowly. He saw the dark grey shadow of his uncle over by the door though he didn't see his face.

'I can't do this without you, Toby. I won't be able to do it alone. Will you help me? Will you trust and help me? Will you believe I'm on your side?'

Toby looked up. His eyes stung. Somehow it was all still like a dream. He could just make out his uncle's face now, it was growing lighter all the time. 'I'll try,' he whispered. He thought he could catch the ghost of a smile on his uncle's face but he wasn't sure. There was a shuffling of paper.

'I. . . wondered if you might read the story that I found in Luxor,' uncle Nichol said rather carefully, getting to his feet. 'Don't worry, I've translated it into English! Would you. . . do that?'

'It's still only early in the morning,' Toby grumbled, pulling the bedclothes tighter round his shoulders. He was sure it couldn't be more than six or seven.

'All right then. I have to go upstairs and start looking at

36

my plans for the rocket. You get some more sleep and when you feel up to it have a read of this. And remember, every word of it is true. Now what day is it?'

'Thursday, the twenty-eighth,' Toby said at once.

'That means we have two days – two days and a great deal to do. I'm going to need your help, you know – I can't begin to tell you how much I'll need it. By the way,' he finished shyly, 'd'you prefer to be called Toby or Daniel?'

'I don't mind you calling me Daniel,' Toby mumbled and lay back down in the warm cocoon of the bed. He heard his uncle placing the manuscript he'd been holding at the bottom of the bed; he could hear it crinkling when he wiggled his toes. It was like Christmas morning when he knew his dad had left his stocking at the bottom of his bed and he wondered just what might lie inside.

He tried to go back to sleep but realised in the end that it was too late, that he was wide awake. The room was brighter now, but as cold as a snowball. He had to count down from sixty before he found the courage to throw off the quilt and the blankets and get up. He dressed in about twenty-three and a half seconds.

He opened the curtains and gasped at what he saw. The snow lay like a white blanket under his window and everything was glittering in the first bright light of the sun. The clouds in the east were all orange and pink, and light turned the snow the most wonderful golden-red. He stood there for a long time just leaning his elbows on the windowsill. This was the kind of winter he had been dreaming of. . .

For a minute he wished he could go off sledging. There were any number of good places round about and after the frost last night. . . But he remembered that he had work to do and he turned round sadly and sighed.

Somewhere called the Little Moon. . . an expedition in Roman times. . . a manuscript from Egypt! All of it seemed to make the maddest story he'd ever heard in his life. But what made him wonder was his uncle's way of working. Toby knew that everything had to be proved to him before his uncle would believe. He was very fair but he was also very strict when it came to science. One doubt was one too many. Toby was amazed at just how much his uncle believed in all of this.

He sat on his bed and picked up the manuscript. Suddenly the sun's red light poured into the room and almost blinded him. Red sky in the morning – maybe that meant there was going to be more snow that day? Oh, he hoped so. He had difficulty reading his uncle's scribbled words – there were lots of scorings out and question marks. The original words in Latin were so beautiful; every single letter was clear.

'Ten leagues from Tiberius I met the ancient man in
his white villa on the summit of the great hill. It was
February, the final day of this leap year – the twenty-
ninth. He said almost nothing to me before nightfall
came. He was very agitated, ran this way and that,
fetching strange objects that he set in the domed
room from which he observed the heavens. Gradually
the daylight faded and the stars began to form like
magnificent jewels. By good fortune it had been a
clear and beautiful day; the moon rose at last into the
sky like a great coin and turned pure gold. By this
time the old man's hands were trembling and his eyes

darting this way and that. He put my eye to a long dark pole with what seemed like a crystal at its end. I found I was looking at the moon, and yet it was far larger than I had seen it before – a great gold disc that seemed huge as a shield. But it was not clear; the crystal through which I observed it made its surface appear blurred and smooth. Yet all that was forgotten as I saw something else – a dark circle that passed across the face of the moon, a small thing that was nonetheless clear and real.

"The Little Moon," the old man breathed.

'Only a few heartbeats and then it was past, lost in the darkness of the skies above Tiberius. I found that my own hands were trembling too, and I asked the old man what this strange sight might be. He told me that it appeared only this once every four years, on the twenty-ninth of February. Long years before he had found it by accident in the skies and had resolved to visit it. He had laboured diligently to make a wind machine that would propel him into the skies with sufficient force to reach the Little Moon. He had calculated the precise distance it would be necessary to travel and the time it would take him to reach the Little Moon. He had been fearful and yet his whole life seemed bent now to this one purpose. In that very place he had built the ship that would carry him and had begun gathering the engines he required. On February the twenty-ninth his ship was propelled into

the skies and at length he came in safety to the Little
Moon. It was while he was there he discovered a
handful of dust. . . '

Toby searched for more of his uncle's translation. It looked
as if the original Latin manuscript went on longer. That was
strange. But the story of the first voyage to the Little Moon
was so clear in his mind. He could see the mountain-top and
the strange craft bursting into the sky. But what were wind
machines?

He got up and went out of his bedroom, listened on the
landing to hear where uncle Nichol might be. Sure enough,
sounds were coming from the attic. Toby took the stairs two
by two and popped his head up at last into the domed ceiling
of the house. Now he could see the rocket all right. It was
much brighter than when he'd last stood here and one side
of the rocket shone dully. Then Toby saw his uncle hanging
upside down from a little ladder, fixing something on close
to the top. He looked very silly indeed with all his silvery hair
splayed out beneath his head – a bit like a carrot with grey
roots. Toby couldn't help but giggle, but he realised that his
uncle was looking straight at him and he didn't want to appear
rude. Then the head suddenly turned the right way up.

'Did you know that I trained for six months with the
Moscow State Circus, Daniel?'

Toby looked at him with wide eyes.

'Come on up here to the platform. Don't worry, you won't
fall. Yes, I had been thrown out of university and I was off
seeing the world. I landed up in Moscow in the very middle
of winter without so much as a decent coat. And you know

how I survived?' Toby shook his head. He climbed with great care onto the platform on which his uncle was standing and grabbed hold of the metal railing on the rocket. 'I slept at the back of a baker's! It was wonderfully warm, but the only thing was that I felt hungry all the time. The smell of bread and cakes morning, noon and night, and I didn't have so much as a kopek to spend!'

Toby suddenly realised he felt hungry himself, but he tried to push the thought of food to the back of his mind. He remembered something. 'The story of the first journey to the Little Moon. Was there more? The part I was reading just stopped in the middle of a sentence. . .'

His uncle started busying himself with something on the side of the rocket. 'Oh, you read the main part, Daniel. And isn't it an amazing story? I meant to tell you that I spoke to your mother early this morning.'

Toby's heart lifted. 'How is she?'

'Yes, she sounded bright. But she's longing to be allowed home. They're good to her in hospital but it can never be the same as being at home. For one thing she doesn't sleep well. But she sent you her love, Daniel, and told me to tell you your father is looking at a new house in Lanark today.' Uncle Nichol was trying to reach some vent or other low down on the rocket and twisting himself into the most amazing shape. Toby couldn't help but giggle again.

'Can I help you?' he asked.

'No,' his uncle, said, giving up trying to reach the vent, all out of breath. 'But you can do some maths for me, Daniel. That's where I really need your help.'

He climbed down from the platform, over to the side of

41

the attic. All at once Toby caught the familiar eyes of Malice at the top of the staircase. They were glimmering like yellow gemstones in the pale light. She gave a long, forlorn meow.

'No, you're not coming to the Little Moon!' uncle Nichol said firmly, squatting down to open the folder Toby had first seen when he sneaked up to the attic that first morning. Slowly Toby's eyes got used to the gloom and he took in the intricacy of his uncle's drawings.

'How's the rocket powered?' he asked.

'I'm glad you asked me that!' uncle Nichol said. He sat down cross-legged on the floorboards, holding one of the drawings up in front of his nephew. 'Whenever I read about these wind machines in the Latin manuscript I get excited. I knew that somehow or other that man had managed to catch the wind and use it to power his ship! That was why it was so important they were high up, right on top of the mountain, where the winds would be fiercest. As soon as I got back from Egypt I started experimenting – I've been working and working on the idea for the last two years. The rocket was really the easy bit, but getting it powered was what took so long.' He put down the drawing very carefully, along with the others. Malice appeared like a ghostly black shadow, purring, and rubbed herself against his back. Uncle Nichol spoke very carefully, in a loud whisper, as if he was afraid someone was listening to him.

'What I did was to create special vents all round the roof. Last autumn we seemed to have one gale after another, and by then I'd devised a way of storing the power.' He leaned close to Toby. 'Can you believe it? The rods underneath the rocket that aren't much bigger than your hands are filled with a whole winter's wind?' He shifted on the floorboards. 'But what I need you to do, Daniel, is to work out precisely when we need to blast off in order to land on the Little Moon as it crosses our moon's orbit. That will be at midnight. Now, here are all the figures for the rocket's speed and the distance I estimate the Little Moon to be from our earth. D'you think you can do that?'

Toby wasn't sure. But he found himself nodding all the same.

6. The Preparations

Somewhere he had read that the mathematicians long ago had gone into a darkened room, and lain down on the floor, and put a large stone on their stomachs. That was how they concentrated. That was how they came to their answers. Toby had once tried it. It was on the fifth of November. His mum had come into the room to find him like that and she'd just laughed herself silly. He didn't think it had helped much.

'I have to be able to see things in my mind,' he murmured to his uncle suddenly when they were having lunch. His uncle just looked at him, his hair sticking up like the bristles on a kitchen brush. But slowly he seemed to understand.

'I can help you there, Daniel,' he whispered. 'I can help you there.'

After lunch was over he took all the sheets of calculations and put them into a big jotter that he gave to Toby. 'That's yours. Guard it with your life – if you don't then we've lost four whole years.'

He started up the stairs and Toby tried to keep up with him. He was out of breath by the time they reached the attic. Together they stood there, getting their breath back, and uncle Nichol looked up at the ceiling above the rocket. All of a sudden he went over to the left-hand wall and pressed a little button with his forefinger. Still he kept his eye on the ceiling above the rocket. There was a low humming noise and to Toby's amazement they saw that the panels of the roof around the rocket were folding back, one after another. When they had stopped he could see that a circle about two metres wide had opened up in the roof. Already he could feel the cold.

Uncle Nichol looked at him. 'Come on then. Let's get up there.'

Toby looked at him with disbelief in his eyes but uncle Nichol leapt over to the platform around the rocket and began climbing the ladder on the outer side of the rocket. He looked round to see if Toby was following. His eyes were as big as marbles.

'Maybe I'll be struck by lightning a third time,' he whispered.

Toby wasn't sure if he was being very serious indeed or just trying to be funny. He wasn't sure if he should try to find a clever answer or else say nothing at all. He decided to do nothing but follow his uncle. He put the big notebook with all the calculations under his arm and leapt over to the platform. His head was just below his uncle's feet on the ladder.

'Now Daniel, I'll go out first. Wait until I call before you follow me. All right?'

Toby was holding onto the ladder for dear life. All he could do was nod and murmur a very faint 'Yes'. He watched as his uncle scrabbled over the edge of the hole in the roof and disappeared from view. For a few seconds there was no sign of him at all and not so much as a single sound.

Toby began to panic. It felt as if the book under his arm was beginning to slip. He heard a loud meow beneath him and looked down to see yellow eyes in the blackness of the attic. Malice had followed them up there. Suddenly Toby wondered what was going to happen to Malice, Tweedledum and Tweedledee, not to mention the goats, while they were away on the Little Moon. Surely uncle Nichol hadn't forgotten about them? But what if they never came back?

'Da-niel!'

He looked up sharply and saw his uncle leaning over and peering down at him. There was a ring of sunlight around his head. He was extending his arms towards his nephew.

'Give me the calculations! Then I'll haul you up afterwards!'

Toby gave him the precious book and then climbed to the topmost rung of the ladder. He felt strong arms grasp him and in the blink of an eye he was being lifted through the roof of Alumbria into the cold February sunlight. It took his breath away. Everything was crystal clear. It was like being on the top of a hill. His breath clouded away in great billows. Far away in the distance he could see a train snaking away north – all of a sudden he remembered the evening he'd arrived and how little he'd wanted to walk the last of the way to his uncle's. How long ago it all seemed now.

But his uncle didn't appear the least interested in the scenery.

'Now Daniel, d'you see that church spire over to the north-east – there just beside the wood? No, further over, further over! Yes, to the left of the big house. That's it! Now, I remember the first time I saw the Little Moon. I was terribly excited – I came out here onto the roof just as we're doing and I marked the exact point at which the Little Moon reached the middle of the big moon. It was right above that tiny steeple.

Now does that help you?'

Toby nodded. His heart was thumping in his chest but he wasn't quite sure why. But there were calculations humming already in his head like bees.

'All right. I want you to stand exactly here, Daniel. You'll be quite safe – the roof's flat at this bit anyway. But I'll be working on the rocket if you need me – just shout and I'll hear you.'

Toby set to work. He felt good, so good, even though the figures he was working with were enormous and of such importance. He thought of the horrible maths classroom where he normally sat with his ruler and protractor and pencils. Whenever Miss Devlin went out Billy Cartwright would come up behind him and poke his ruler in Toby's back.

'Teacher's pet! Posh swot, Toby Goodwin! Let's get his answers then, boys!'

Billy Cartwright would grab his jotter and chuck it round the class from each of the bullies to the next. Toby didn't bother chasing after it; there was no point. He just sat there, staring straight ahead at the blackboard with his arms folded, as Billy Cartwright pushed him from behind and the others hooted and copied down the answers to Miss Devlin's most difficult questions. There was always one girl who watched him then, Toby noticed. Samantha Brown. She looked round from where she sat at the front and stared straight at him. She never said anything to defend him and she never smiled at him – she just looked straight at him. That was all.

But this was different. His fingers were so cold he could hardly write, but in a way that was all right, it didn't matter. He enjoyed forming each number with the sharp point of the pencil, he loved the curve of each one. There was no need to hurry, there was no Billy Cartwright to fear. This answer would be all his own; it wouldn't be thrown about from desk to desk for everyone to steal.

A tiny edge of breeze fluttered against his cheek and he shivered. He stopped and looked all round him – it was still early in the morning and Scotland seemed asleep. He looked behind him, back towards Edinburgh, and the grey line of buildings that stretched across the horizon far away. Somewhere in among all that mess of bricks and slates and streets was his mother. For a moment even the sums he had to work out for his uncle were forgotten, didn't matter any more. She was the only thing that mattered. But he had to trust uncle Nichol all the same, believe that somehow he really was doing this for her. And so he had to do this for her too.

Somehow or other when Toby concentrated on a maths question he could shut out absolutely everything else. It was like banging lots of doors and going right into the very centre of his head. In there it was utterly silent, and he was totally alone. But although he was alone he never felt lonely. That was the funny thing, although he was alone he was not lonely, absolutely not. It felt the best thing in the world. He worked now and the figures flowed over the page in front of him and he got closer and closer to the solution. It didn't feel frightening any more. He knew he had the right answer – not in some cocky way, not like that, but he just knew all the same. And when he was finished he had no idea if ten minutes had passed or ten whole hours.

'Will you be sleeping out here tonight?'

His uncle's voice made him all but jump into the air.

'No,' he smiled. 'I've finished.' He looked at his figures a final time and his words were slow and careful as he read them. 'I've worked out that we'll have to leave at exactly twenty-five minutes to six tomorrow evening. Any later and it's useless.' Uncle Nichol stretched his arm through the hole in the attic roof and clasped his hand.

'Well done, boy!' he whispered. 'Well done. I told you I needed you!'

It was only once he'd climbed back down into the house that he realised just how cold he was. His hands were blue. But it didn't matter. He had done it!

7. The Final Day

'By the way Daniel, I didn't tell you that Mrs MacPherson would be coming over this afternoon.'

It was lunch and the two of them were chewing dry bits of German bread. Malice was looking up at them as if she could cast spells. Toby didn't say anything but gave his uncle a hard look. Who on earth was Mrs MacPherson? Uncle Nichol bothered very little about other human beings and for the most part found them a nuisance. Mrs MacPherson?

'She. . . ah. . . lives in the village and has. . . ah. . . done the odd spot of, you know, baby-sitting while I'm away.'

Uncle Nichol had gone an odd red colour.

'Baby-sitting? You don't have a baby!'

'No, I have three goats, two very bouncy dogs and a very miserable cat. Why am I having to defend myself?'

Toby realised that it wouldn't be wise to push this any further. He washed up without being asked. But when he came out into the hall ten minutes later a rather large lady was coming in. She hadn't rung the bell and she was carrying several enormous plastic bags.

'Mr Randolph, you can't be thinking of going away at the end of February when the country's in the grip of an Ice Age. Are you out of your senses? What about the plumbing? I know nothing about plumbing, you know. I can't even change a plug.'

His uncle was standing tight against the hall wall, his hair more on end than ever. In fact it looked to Toby as if he'd been struck by lightning for a third time. He wanted to go and rescue his uncle, but changed his mind at the last minute. He was enjoying this far too much. Very seldom had he seen his uncle lost for words. Mrs MacPherson plonked down one bag and tipped out a whole collection of keys – brass keys, silver keys and great rusty keys. His uncle started to open his mouth and seemed to Toby at that moment not unlike a stuffed goldfish. His hands were pinned to the wall.

'And where are you going tomorrow evening with your poor nephew, Mr Randolph? Where is it this time? Are you off on another one of your ludicrous scientific trips?' She looked up from among the collection of keys and suddenly screwed up her eyes. 'Is that the shirt I carefully ironed for you two Saturdays ago?' She lunged at him rather like a hen going for a worm and he sprang backwards.

'Mrs MacPherson, I haven't spoiled it, I can assure you. And we're not going far, in fact we should be back the day after tomorrow. I'd just be grateful if you might look after the animals for that time, please.'

Toby came out of hiding. Mrs MacPherson caught sight of him and beamed at him, her face bright as a sunrise. His uncle crawled up the side of the wall.

'And so you must be Toby?' she said, her voice full of gentle warmth. She extended her hand to shake his.

'I've heard so much about you, Toby.'

'I'm very pleased to meet you, Mrs MacPherson. I'm sorry, I was just in the kitchen doing the washing up.'

'Oh, what a good boy! But to think your uncle's making

you work!' He shrank again as she gave him a furious look. 'Now you see that you're looked after just as a guest should be,' she went on, coming over towards him and straightening his collar. 'And if you aren't you can come right up the village street and tell me the reason why, d'you hear me? Right, I'd better go and see to those brasses.'

She vanished into the living room, another bag under her arm. Uncle Nichol picked himself up and Toby almost tied himself in knots with laughter. All of a sudden Mrs Mac-Pherson's head reappeared round the side of the door. Uncle Nichol looked as if he had been bitten by a poisonous snake.

'And what time are you leaving tomorrow?' she demanded.

'Half past five, Mrs MacPherson,' Toby said, since he could see that his uncle was completely speechless. 'Half past five in the evening.'

'You won't need to come in until the following morning,' uncle Nichol whispered.

Mrs MacPherson gave him a fiery look and vanished again.

'I'm going to hide in the attic,' uncle Nichol hissed. 'I want you to have a look at what the weather's doing. When the coast's clear, come up and join me.' Toby was all set to ask something, but his uncle was already taking the stairs two by two. He suddenly remembered what his mother had once told him when he was laughing a bit at his mad uncle:

'That brother of mine never had a single friend when he was a boy, Toby. He didn't know how to make friends. He was far better with animals and machines than with people. They didn't answer back or make fun of him.'

Toby stood there for a moment, thinking. He could hear Mrs MacPherson from where he was standing, tutting at something and mumbling a whole string of thoughts even though she was quite on her own. Was that why uncle Nichol had chosen to come to Alumbria in the end? Because it was the safest place in the world?

He padded out quietly into the porch and looked up at the skies. He wasn't sure why his uncle was the least bit worried about the weather right at that moment, but still.

It was clear and cold, hardly a cloud in the skies. Toby was sure it was going to freeze and that would mean the snow would last another day. He cheered inside.

When he tiptoed back inside he glanced round into the living room to see where Mrs MacPherson was. He was just in time to see Malice stretch up on her back legs and dig ten claws into the back of her left leg. Mrs MacPherson screeched and Malice fled like a streak of black lightning. So did Toby. He went as quiet as a mouse up the various sets of stairs until he found his uncle huddled in the attic.

'Is she gone yet?' he asked miserably.

Toby told him what Malice had done and a thin smile appeared on his lips.

'Good,' he whispered. 'I call that woman the Tartan Terror.'

Uncle Nichol had a secret kettle hidden up in the attic and they warmed themselves with a piping hot mug of tea after closing the hole in the roof above the rocket. Toby gave his uncle a clear description of the weather conditions.

'That's good too, Daniel. Were you able to see the moon?'

Toby was more and more puzzled. What was his uncle thinking? Was he planning on leaving early for the Little Moon? Surely Mrs MacPherson, the Tartan Terror, couldn't have frightened him that much? But his uncle would say very little indeed. He sat on the floorboards, hunched over, his white hair standing on end all over his head. He seemed to be lost in his own world, almost as if he forgot Toby was there at all. And Toby felt it was hard to believe that this was the same person that had talked with such great excitement about the journey that was to take place on the 29th, the person who had rushed about the rocket beginning to get everything ready.

'I want to do some work with the air vents,' he suddenly said to Toby and turned to look at him. 'You go off down and see what that dreadful woman's doing. See she doesn't set fire to anything.'

Toby couldn't help but feel that his uncle wanted to get

rid of him but he had no choice but to go all the same.

'May I phone mum?' he asked before he started down the stairs.

His uncle's eyes softened. 'You phone your mother any time you want,' he said, pointing at him with a screwdriver. It sounded more like an order than anything else, but it made Toby feel all warm inside, even though he didn't quite know why. In the end it was difficult to hear anything much on the other end of the line because Mrs MacPherson was dragging chairs about and singing rather badly. His mother said she was tired, but he managed to make her laugh too when he told her what Malice had done to Mrs MacPherson, and that had to be a good sign. All of a sudden Toby wanted to tell her about the rocket, the journey, but at the last moment the words went dry in his mouth. He just told her about the snow instead; the snow and that wonderful bath he'd had on the first morning. He didn't quite know why but he felt he shouldn't say anything about the rocket. He heard his mother saying goodbye in the end and the line went dead, began humming in that way which always made him feel frightened, even though he never quite knew why. This was his adventure now, uncle Nichol's and his alone.

He was still sitting thinking in the living room ten minutes later when Mrs MacPherson put her head round the door to say she was all done in the house.

'You'll catch your death of cold in here, Toby! Can that old miser not even afford to put a fire on for you? Now make sure he looks after you all right when you're away, d'you hear me? And I'll see you both on March the first.'

The front door banged and the house was completely still.

The only sound was the ticking of the ancient clock in the hall. Toby suddenly remembered again how frightened he'd been of the house when he was younger. It didn't help when his uncle looked at him, his grey hair sticking up in all directions, and told him ghost stories.

'Daniel!' He got such a fright he almost jumped out of his skin. His uncle laughed, but not as much as he might normally have done. He was more thoughtful, quieter. It was almost as if he was sad about something, but Toby couldn't quite tell what it was that was making him that way.

'I want you to come with me, Daniel. You're not hungry, are you? Is it all right if we eat when we come back?'

His uncle was getting ready to go out and it was already almost dark. Toby had no choice but to put on his own things too. Where on earth were they going now?

His uncle told him to wait while he got something from the shed. While he was away, Toby made a fuss of Tweedledum and Tweedledee, who were standing in the porch. Their hot breath rose up in great silver clouds.

He heard his uncle coming back with something. It was the toboggan, the sledge the two dogs had pulled the evening before. But this time Tweedledum and Tweedledee weren't coming with them; uncle Nichol pointed in a different direction but wouldn't say where it was they were going. It was getting darker every minute, but if anything the night was colder than any they'd had before that winter. The snow was crisp and shone like jewels, and the great curve of the moon was just beginning to rise into the sky.

Uncle Nichol didn't say anything at all as he strode on. Toby wondered at first if he was annoyed by something he'd done – was it because of the way he'd been with Mrs MacPherson? He tried to think of things to say but his mouth went all dry and funny, and he kept forgetting what he wanted to say. He felt nervous and his heart began hammering in his chest. They started climbing a small hill and Toby thought back to the mammoth sum he'd worked out on the roof of the house that day. It comforted him to think of it, to imagine the numbers going through his head. He scrambled as fast as he could through deep grass and over boulders, trying to keep up with his uncle. He looked strange, his long coat billowing out behind him and his silver hair lit by the moonlight. The sledge thumped and banged behind him.

Then all of a sudden they were there, on top of a little hill. Toby glanced round and could see Alumbria behind them, the porch light still shining out over the snow. Except now it looked like a toy house, a doll's house. He put his hands on his knees and tried to get his breath back.

'Are you frightened, Daniel?'

His uncle didn't sound out of breath in the least.

Toby had to think for a minute. 'What d'you mean?' he asked. Uncle Nichol didn't look at him. He had his hands buried deep in the pockets of his great coat, and in his left hand he held the rope for the toboggan.

'Are you frightened of the journey?'

He hadn't thought of that before; it hadn't really entered his head to be frightened of it. He had felt *excited* when he first found out about the rocket, nothing but excited. Not frightened, certainly not frightened. He wasn't always sure if he really believed it was all going to happen – he'd seen the rocket all right, he knew it was real, yet somehow the journey itself still seemed somehow too unbelievable, too mad to be true.

'Not yet,' he said at last. Then he dared to say something else. 'Why do you ask me that?'

His uncle was quiet for a moment.

'Because I'm frightened, Daniel. I've never been anywhere in the rocket and though I've dreamed and dreamed of travelling to the Little Moon now I feel frightened. I know I have to go, and I have to take you with me, but I'm afraid all the same. I look up at that moon and I think to myself that tomorrow night we'll be heading for that moon's little brother. If we make it we'll be looking down at this place instead. And even though I'm a scientist and know I've done everything the right way I still sometimes feel afraid. Because doing something like this takes faith, Daniel. D'you understand what I mean? D'you know what faith is?'

Toby nodded. He had a lump in his throat. He'd looked at his mother in her hospital bed and tried to have faith, faith that she'd get better, even though she was so very ill.

'You see we might not make it back, Daniel,' uncle Nichol whispered, and for the first time he turned to look at his nephew. Then Toby saw that uncle Nichol's right hand was stretched out towards him, and he reached out with his own hand to hold it. He thought his uncle was smiling to him in the darkness.

'But I believe we will,' uncle Nichol whispered, and gave his hand a squeeze.

'Now come on, I didn't bring you all this way up here just to make you depressed.'

8. The Birthday

Uncle Nichol sat down at the front of the sledge and looked round to make sure Toby found the best position. They edged towards the top of the slope and Toby had a flickering view of the hill they were about to descend. He opened his mouth but no sound came – it looked impossibly steep.

Then he felt the dark wind rushing past his ears and all he could hear was the hissing of the runners on the snow as they curved to one side and then plunged down the next descent. He hung on to his uncle for dear life, and maybe now he was shrieking aloud, but he couldn't hear himself. He saw trees ahead and uncle Nichol swerved to one side; the steepest part of the hill seemed to be past now and Toby glanced up to see the moon flickering past the trees. This was the kind of sledge-run he'd dreamed of all his life but never known. Every winter he'd looked out of the Edinburgh windows and hoped, prayed, that there might be enough to last till Saturday, that it might freeze hard. But the world always turned grey again, went back to rain.

Now he was shrieking, but not in terror, rather in sheer delight – and uncle Nichol was shrieking with him. Toby looked up at the clear and silver face of the moon with all its valleys and craters, and he thought to himself that the following night he'd be hurtling towards that moon at a speed that didn't even bear thinking about. This was nothing, this was the tiniest fraction of it. But he tried to think in that moment of nothing else but the sledge-run; he tried to stop worrying about all that uncle Nichol had said about the possibility of not coming back at all. Because this was the winter he'd been dreaming of all his life, and it was happening right at the time of his birthday – the day before February the 29th. And all he thought of instead was how very strange life is, how impossible it is to predict anything at all. He thought of just how he'd felt sitting on that train only a few days before. . .

Uncle Nichol swerved at the last moment and swung round too sharply – there was a loud thud as they banged into a tree stump, and Toby found himself spinning round like a snowball and landing flat on his back. He was looking straight up at the moon and he was laughing and laughing.

Eventually uncle Nichol's face appeared above him.

'Are you all right, Daniel?' he asked, his voice worried.

Toby tried to sit up on his elbows and couldn't make it. He slumped back down again.

'That was the most wonderful sledge-run ever,' he said.

'Well, I'm afraid it's a long way home,' his uncle told him.

But it didn't matter. When they got there they had roast pheasant and piping hot potatoes and a sweet the recipe of which uncle Nichol said was as old as Julius Caesar (he had found it in a book and translated it from Latin). It tasted strange, of chestnuts and figs and cream. And best of all, Toby had a glass of his uncle's homemade ginger beer. It was so strong it took your breath away.

Uncle Nichol raised his own glass, 'This is to a very happy birthday,' he said. 'Despite all the other things that may be difficult or worrying, I'm glad you're here.'

And so are you, Malice, aren't you?'

Toby thanked his uncle as he fought to get a piece of fig out from between two teeth with his tongue.

'When did you learn to cook so well?' he asked, frowning.

'Flattery, my dear boy, will get you everywhere. I learned when I was in Moscow, during my six months with the State Circus. I was taught by a girl called Irina.'

A strange look crossed uncle Nichol's face and he took a very long drink of ginger beer. Toby wondered for a while whether or not he should ask any more and decided in the end it would be wisest not to.

He was so tired by ten o'clock that he had no choice but to trail off upstairs to bed, leaving uncle Nichol and Malice in the living room. He glanced out of his bedroom window at the white world under the moonlight and thought about the sledge run. He would never forget it.

During the night Toby was sure he heard noises from somewhere above him, and the sound of a strange rushing wind. But he woke up before it had properly grown light and lay on his back thinking. It was the twenty-ninth of February. His birthday. He suddenly wondered what it must be like for all the others around the world who shared his birthday. Did they feel the same? Had they been made fun of at school too?

Then he felt a strange warmth, a glowing, deep inside. For they would never know about the Little Moon, and that it too appeared only once every four years. It was as though it was appearing especially to wish him a happy birthday.

At eight o'clock he padded downstairs to the phone. He wished so much he could see his mother today, on his birthday. He wished it so much it made his eyes sting with tears. He called her, but even though they laughed together, Toby got the feeling that somehow her laughter hurt. He couldn't tell quite why or how, but that was how he felt all the same. She sounded very, very far away and somehow he felt that her voice was white. Before he put down the receiver, she told him that his dad was looking at a house that day in a village north of Glasgow. He'd tried to phone, but it wasn't certain he'd get a signal on his mobile. They both sent all their love on his birthday. Then she was gone. Alumbria was silent and full of shadows. Tony padded upstairs, his bare feet making not a sound.

Not long afterwards there was a knock on the door. Uncle Nichol came in, carrying a plate with a funny-shaped lump of cake on it. And in the middle of the lump of cake there was a lighted candle. Uncle Nichol sat down at the end of the bed. Toby thought he looked tired.

'That's the Little Moon,' he whispered, pointing to the cake. 'It's covered in craters because so many meteorites have left their marks on its surface. And the candle's our mark, Daniel, our flag. Happy Birthday.'

Uncle Nichol put down a small cylindrical-shaped present beside his nephew. He nodded when Toby wasn't sure whether to open it or not. He kept his eyes on the present all the time. It was heavy, as heavy as lead or gold. Toby couldn't think what in the world it could be. He unwrapped the object as carefully as he could because his mother had always told him not to tear the paper.

'That present's from all of us – your mum and dad and me,' uncle Nichol said.

Toby gasped as he saw that it was a real telescope in a

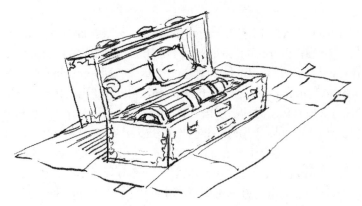

beautiful chestnut leather case. It was old, but the glass in it was perfectly clear, absolutely smooth and undamaged.

'I found it in an antique shop in London,' uncle Nichol said. 'The man who sold it to me told me it had been taken on one of the first expeditions to the Antarctic. It belonged to the astronomer, the one who was going to look at the southern skies. So that telescope has been all the way to the South Pole, Daniel.'

Toby didn't know what to say. Thank you just didn't seem enough. He simply looked at his uncle, that was all he seemed able to do. But uncle Nichol seemed to understand all right. He smiled and ruffled his hair.

'Just promise me you'll never let a birthday go past without looking for the Little Moon,' he said.

'I promise,' Toby whispered.

'And the rest of the day is your own, young man. This is your birthday and I want you to enjoy all you can of it. I'm going to have to get our things ready and make sure the rocket's ship-shape, so I'm afraid you're going to have to spend most of the time on your own. But I expect you're used to that,' he added, in a softer voice.

Uncle Nichol left him on his own and he lay there a bit longer, holding the telescope in his hands. The first thing he did was to work out how many days he'd been alive for. It seemed such a long time. Then he thought of the story uncle Nichol had found of the first visit to the Little Moon, and he imagined just how many days had passed since then. He went over to the window and saw to his delight that it was snowing again – there wasn't so much as a breath of wind and it was snowing heavily. What if each snowflake was one day? How long before enough snowflakes had fallen to make up the days that had passed since the first landing on the Little Moon? But then he got lost completely and he realised he was getting cold. A robin landed on the windowsill and looked at him with its head on one side. He decided the first real thing he'd do on his birthday would be to go out with a little bit of his cake and share it with the robin. He just wished it could be with his mum.

Toby got dressed and went downstairs, and out over to the trees. He found the secret path between them, and came into the clearing where uncle Nichol's tower was.

He went inside and climbed the staircase to the very highest level to the little chamber his uncle used for watching the stars. Toby lay down on his back and looked up at the dome of the skies in the glass roof, and he cried and he cried and he cried. There was no-one to hear him except himself, and when he stopped he suddenly felt better, as if something had gone. The part of him that had hurt so badly was still not right, but it was right for now.

He remembered that the day was his. He decided that he'd make a snow alien, someone they might encounter on the Little Moon. It had huge eyes made of tennis balls, and sticky up ears he made out of old bits of wood. When he stood back and looked at it he laughed himself silly. He decided it actually looked more like a girl called Clare Adam in his class in Edinburgh. She always seemed very worried, and what he'd made looked like her after she'd had a terrible fright.

Next he decided to go and pay the goats a visit. The Three Wise Men looked at him with big eyes; Toby reached out his hand to scratch the bit above their noses.

'So have you worked out how far it is to the Little Moon, Caspar?' he whispered, and bent down to look the goat in the eyes. If Caspar knew, he was saying nothing. It was warm in the shed and Toby stayed there a while, listening to the soft movements of the goats on their chains as they munched their breakfast. He liked tugging the long white curl of their beards.

After that Toby read one of the books he'd brought with him from home, and got himself some lunch in the kitchen. He took the sledge out with him for a bit, and went back to the run that he and his uncle had done the evening before. It was still fun, yet somehow not quite the same as by moonlight, or without uncle Nichol. When the sledge finally stopped he sat there thinking about something he hadn't really considered before. Things were never quite the same the second time round; you couldn't ever make it quite like the first time. You would always hope it could be, but it wouldn't happen. Then just as he was struggling up onto his feet, Toby realised that he was scared. It came to him in a flash. He was scared of the journey!

9. The Journey

He just sat there, the sledge behind him at the end of its string, listening to his heart thudding in his chest. He looked up and he saw that already it was beginning to get dark. There was the moon, high up and as pale as a ball of cobwebs. Soon the sky round it would turn dark blue and then black as night fell.

Twenty-five to six. That complicated sum he'd worked out himself, up there on the roof of Alumbria. And it wasn't just some time in the future now, it wasn't just a rather exciting idea at the back of the mind that you could think about from time to time without really worrying about – it was a reality. He swallowed. It was an absolute certainty. And it was tonight. He shivered.

Toby ran back the whole way to the house. He was a year older, but the reality was that he felt a year younger. He felt small and scared. He got to the porch door and heard Tweedledum and Tweedledee scrabbling about somewhere in the shadows. A mad thought flashed across his mind. What if he were to leave everything and go to the station right now, right that minute? He could be back in Edinburgh by early evening and he could go to the hospital! Uncle Nichol would be all right on his own, he'd cope fine. It was his crazy idea to do all this anyway, so why shouldn't he do it himself? Just for a split second Toby actually thought of running away, of going back to Edinburgh.

But he couldn't. How on earth would he explain everything to his mother? And he couldn't let uncle Nichol down; he was relying on him, he'd said that he needed him. With a heavy heart he went back inside. There in the porch he saw the telescope that his uncle had given him for his birthday and he felt ashamed. He would take the telescope with him. He picked it up and held it tightly in his hands. All he needed was courage. He looked at the hall clock and saw that it was twenty-four minutes past four. It felt suddenly like sitting waiting for the dentist, knowing the minutes were slipping by one by one – hearing them slipping by. He found himself going upstairs as if in a dream; he felt dizzy and had to hold on to the banister. When he reached the attic he was out of breath; uncle Nichol was fixing something on the nose of the rocket and the window in the roof above was open. The skies were deep blue, beginning to darken. He felt excited and frightened at one and the same time and he wasn't sure if he was freezing cold or trembling. Uncle Nichol suddenly realised he was there and looked round.

'Good day?' he asked, smiling.

Guiltily Toby remembered what he'd just been thinking, that somehow he could run away from Alumbria and not face the journey at all.

He smiled back and nodded.

'I'm glad,' his uncle said, climbing down from the top of the rocket. 'Well, we've one hour and ten minutes. I want you to go and dress as warmly as you can, Daniel. I've left some clothes out for you in the bedroom and I want you to wear every stitch of them.' He reached the bottom of the ladder and jumped over from the platform. 'It's very important we dress right. Then come back and help me with the last things.'

There was a vest and horrible woollen underwear that scratched terribly when Toby pulled it on. It felt as though ants were going up and down his legs and he made the most awful face. There were thick woollen stockings too and a big furry hat like the ones he'd seen Russian politicians wearing. He looked at himself in the mirror.

'I'm very glad to meet you, comrade general,' he said to his reflection in his best Russian accent. He pulled off the hat and looked at it. No doubt uncle Nichol had got it when he trained for those six months with the Moscow State Circus.

Finally there was a huge long coat that trailed down to his ankles. He felt the sweat tickling his forehead. He looked as if he was going to a fancy dress party, not on a lunar expedition. He tramped back upstairs to the attic, taking care not to trip over the coat. But uncle Nichol didn't laugh when he saw him.

'You don't need to wear the coat just now,' he said, 'but I do want you to take it with you. And there are gloves inside the pockets. I'm going to go and change myself now. You can start stowing some of the boxes in the bottom compartment, Daniel. There's a full medical kit there, some provisions, and two containers of fresh water. Pack them as tightly as you can.'

'What about oxygen?' Toby asked. How would they breathe?

'The rocket has its own air system, like a plane. On the Little Moon it'll be thin, but there'll be air. We just have to be careful not to move too quickly when we're there, that's all.'

Forty-five minutes to go. Toby packed the boxes and noticed that his hands were shaking. The rocket looked so small; he wondered how on earth he would stand being cramped there for more that six hours. He saw that inside there were two chambers, one at the front and one behind. The one at the front contained all sorts of dials and levers – it was bewilderingly complicated. And a thick wall of glass lined the top, hard as granite. Suddenly the thought went through his mind with extraordinary calmness – *this is the most exciting moment of my whole life*.

He remembered being on holiday somewhere – perhaps it had been the west coast of Ireland – looking up at the night sky in the middle of the summer. He'd never seen so many stars properly before because it was so difficult to see them in Edinburgh. He'd looked up and wished with all his heart he could go there, to one of the stars. He wanted to know what it would be like to look back down at the tiny dot of the earth. But never in all his wildest dreams had he imagined it might really happen.

Thirty-five minutes. He heard his uncle coming back up the stairs and he couldn't help bursting out laughing when he saw him. It was the hat. He had on a brown leather hat with side flaps rather like the things pilots used to wear back in the early days of flying. His uncle didn't look angry at all, perhaps just a little embarrassed.

'Well, at least we aren't going to meet anyone else up there,' he said gently. 'Now, I'm going to show you something of the controls, Daniel. Just in case anything happens to me.'

Toby didn't know what to say but he had no choice but to

follow uncle Nichol. He tried to listen to what he was told about the difference between red and green levers, the correct way of operating certain functions, the timing of particular operations. He tried his best to concentrate but his mind was racing. When his uncle asked him if he had any questions his mouth felt so dry he could only shake his head in reply.

The clock downstairs in the hall struck a quarter past five. Twenty minutes. He went over the sum his uncle had asked him to work out the previous day. What if he'd made some terrible mistake? But no, it was the same result he reached. Twenty-five to six.

'I nearly forgot!' uncle Nichol exclaimed. All Toby could see of him was his bottom; he was pulling some long piece of material from one of the trunks over by the door. He turned round in triumph, grinning from ear to ear.

'This is the Randolph flag,' he said. 'Designed by me in 1987, the first year I came to Alumbria.' He held it up in front of him, unfurled it. 'There's the house in the middle, see. And the library in the trees. And there's the Latin motto below – *sic biscutus disintegrat*. Any idea what that might mean, Daniel?'

His nephew shook his head. No doubt it meant something very grand indeed. But Toby was finding it hard enough to think in English at the moment, let alone anything else.

'That's the way the cookie crumbles!' his uncle said, and roared with laughter at his own joke as he folded the flag into a ball and stuffed it in his pocket. 'You see, I had been hoping to get a quite different house down in Devon, and at the last minute all my plans fell to dust. I was actually quite fed up when I first came here – I thought it was cold and gloomy and dull. So that's why the motto seemed appropriate. Anyway, we'll take this with us and plant it on the Little Moon. Not in the name of the British or the Americans or the Russians, but in the name of the Randolphs. How does that sound to you, Daniel?'

In spite of himself Toby smiled. Ten minutes.

'Right, let's get inside,' his uncle said, his voice softer now. He looked at Toby intently and for a moment the scene was frozen in his mind – the attic, the grey light, the edge of the Randolph flag sticking out of his uncle's pocket. It made him think of one of the huge paintings he'd seen in the London galleries, so detailed you could imagine exactly what the room would have smelled like. He knew he would always remember this moment.

'Wait,' his uncle said suddenly, and Toby could hear his

steps racing down through the house and then he heard his voice, muffled and soft. When he came back, a bit breathless, he didn't look at Toby. He seemed agitated, distracted. Suddenly Toby stretched out his hand and took his uncle's in his own. Shyly he gave it a squeeze.

'Don't worry,' he said. 'We'll see Malice again.'

His uncle just looked away. 'Five minutes, Daniel. We need to get inside. I'll go first. Come after me and close the door as I showed you. We have to start the engines before lift-off and it'll be loud, I warn you. Don't be alarmed. Then, at twenty five to six, we'll be ready. All right?'

His uncle went over to the platform and eased himself up into the higher compartment of the rocket. He gave a sign for Toby to follow. The boy wasn't sure if he could walk. It felt like struggling through deep water. But he found himself folding his head and arms through the tiny opening and squeezing inside. He pulled the metal door behind him and locked it. The rocket was trembling with the shuddering of the engines. Toby thought of the stored power that was being gathered in them. He was breathing too quickly. He had to slow down, he had to calm himself. He closed his eyes as the roaring of the engines became louder than anything he'd ever heard in his life, and then he looked up, into the nose of the rocket, and saw the tiny clock there among all the dials. It was twenty-six minutes to six. The small hand of the dial was moving towards the first quarter; now it had passed the halfway mark, soon it would reach the three-quarters point. With an almighty thunder the rocket burst upwards through the open roof of Alumbria. It was as if it had become so angry it couldn't take any more. The only thing it could do was burst into the skies. It happened so fast that Toby hardly realised anything at all. He caught a glimpse of odd things – a light below them, the sphere of the full moon above, a droplet of water running down the inside of the rocket wall, a strange lightness in his head. He wanted to say something to uncle Nichol and yet he realised that the noise of the rocket would make it impossible.

He looked down again and it was an effort to make his eyes focus; he saw a whole cluster of lights and realised that it was a village, or was it maybe Edinburgh? He felt frightened again, really frightened, and he forced himself to look about him in the rocket. That was something his uncle had told him to do, to concentrate on anything at all round about him. He concentrated on that single droplet of water and watched as it joined up with other drops and ran further and further down. Suddenly he looked up and saw his uncle's face peering down; uncle Nichol didn't say anything but Toby knew he was asking if he was all right. He nodded back. Maybe he smiled; he wasn't sure. There was a ringing in his ears, so much so that he couldn't tell if the engines were very, very loud or growing more silent. Certainly the rocket was moving much less that it had. He looked up again and caught sight of the tiny clock. Was it possible? It was showing almost six o'clock. Had so much time passed already?

He was aware after a bit that the noise of the engines was dying down and for a moment a shadow of fear crossed his heart. What if that meant something was wrong? But then he caught sight of his uncle looking down from the upper part of the rocket, the ghost of a smile on his lips.

'It's all right, Daniel. It's just the first phase passing.'

He nodded, tried to smile.

All of a sudden he remembered something he hadn't thought of for a very, very long time. When he was really young, maybe three or four, his dad used to take them on night drives. He put Toby in the back seat and put a blanket round him. They drove north over the Forth Road Bridge and it looked as though the bridge was made of jewels. It was all lit up white, and when Toby looked down over the river far below he could see all the jewels of the towns on either side, shimmering and glinting. Toby's mum brought a flask with them, a flask of lemon tea, and special chocolate biscuits. They were so exciting, those night drives, and he never wanted his dad to turn round again and head back to Edinburgh.

He suddenly wondered if it would happen again, if the three of them would chat and laugh like that in the future. Somehow he had to believe they would. He wondered why on earth he'd suddenly remembered those journeys now, as they hurtled upwards towards the Little Moon, and he wasn't sure. Maybe it was the distant memory of being strapped into the back seat of the car, although it wasn't much like being in a rocket. Maybe it was the way he saw his uncle from there, even though his uncle and his dad couldn't have been more different.

Slowly the memory faded and the noise of the engines seemed to flood back into his ears. He looked up and saw that another half hour had passed. He felt stiff and wriggled his fingers and toes as uncle Nichol had told him to. He wondered how he'd ever be able to walk by the time they got to the Little Moon.

Suddenly he wondered what would happen if they missed,

if they didn't meet the path of the Little Moon after all and just carried on and on and on into space. . . It was an unbearable thought. His heart thudded so loudly he was sure uncle Nichol would hear it. Would the rocket go on until they were turned to skeletons inside, until even their hands and faces had fallen to dust? He forced himself to stop thinking like that. There was no point; he would drive himself mad in the end! He had to believe the sums he had done on the roof of Alumbria had been right. The only thing there was to do now was to believe.

Suddenly he saw his uncle's face peering down at him again.

'D'you know why my wife left me, Daniel?' he asked, above the roaring of the engines.

Toby's jaw dropped. He'd always thought it was something to do with his uncle not doing the cleaning, that his wife had gone off with the hoover.

He shook his head.

'Because I never came to dinner on time! She couldn't bear the fact that I always came late to the table. And you know Daniel, I'm glad I didn't have to make some kind of excuse this evening!' He laughed aloud. 'That's a great feeling, Daniel, not to worry about going home to get a row for being late for dinner!'

All of a sudden the rocket started shaking violently. Toby reached out with one hand for the side of the craft, as something fell and hit his leg. His heart thundered so loudly he was afraid it might burst – what if this was the end? He glanced up towards his uncle, helpless and terrified, and uncle Nichol was saying something as he looked down at him. But his words were swallowed by the rocking and the engines. Then slowly, very slowly, it started to calm once more.

'It's all right, Daniel, it's nothing to worry about. I should have warned you. It's like passing through a storm on earth, right through the centre of it.'

Toby didn't say anything. He didn't have any words to speak. He was only thankful to be alive; he just sat there looking straight ahead trying to relax his breathing.

'Daniel, look, d'you see? That star – if you look up, ahead of me, right through the nose of the rocket. The star that's winking green and blue and red. D'you know what I find amazing about that star?'

Toby could only shake his head.

'It's been dead for millions of years. When we look at stars like that we're not really seeing them as they are. We're looking at their memories. It's almost like seeing somebody on top of a hill, but because they're far away seeing them as a child, the person they once were, instead of what they are now. People say we can't travel in time, but we can. We can do it whenever we look at the stars. That was one of the reasons I first fell in love with the stars. Because I could be a time traveller.'

'Do you think we'll ever find life somewhere else on some other star?' Toby asked. He was still looking up, forgetting his fear, watching the beautiful jewel sparkling and winking all those millions of miles above him.

'I don't know,' his uncle said softly. 'I really don't know. But what I do know is that we'd have to go a very long way to find it, and that makes me realise just how precious life on earth is.'

When he said those words, Toby suddenly thought of his

mother. For some reason or another he imagined her looking out of her hospital window on to the great white face of the moon, the moon they were hurtling towards. His eyes stung and he was afraid he was going to cry. He felt frightened again, even though the rocket was not shaking.

'How would you like to have your first bit of chocolate in space?' uncle Nichol asked him.

Toby looked up, surprised and stunned.

'There's a box below you and to the left,' his uncle went on. 'That's right, the one with the red lid. There's chocolate in there, and I can tell you that even if there is life on other planets, there certainly won't be chocolate that's half as good as that is!'

Toby smiled in spite of himself. The two of them sat quietly for a time, making the most of their chocolate.

'How many bits are left?' his uncle asked in the end.

'Just two,' Toby told him.

'Hmm. The question is, do we eat them now or wait until we're on the Little Moon? We're either greedy and finish it or else we have those last two bits when we put the Randolph flag in the ground. What d'you say Daniel? You're the one who's going to make the decision!' But he never got his answer. Toby drew in his breath and pointed through the tiny side chink of window, for he'd caught the most magnificent view of a shooting star.

'When you see one you should wish for something,' his uncle told him.

Toby didn't say anything. He was thinking and wishing. Wishing with all his heart.

10. The Little Moon

He must have dozed for a time, quite a while. He dreamed that he was walking towards the end of a great dark corridor. It was completely round and so long he thought he would never reach the far end of it. There were tiny points of light in the dark circle ahead of him and he couldn't work out what they were. Then at last he came to the far end after all and stood on the rim of the circle. He realised that he had been walking through a gigantic telescope and that what he was seeing ahead of him were stars. He began counting them one by one but then there were shooting stars which appeared and disappeared, and he didn't know whether to count them or not. It was the only sum he had ever failed to do and he sat down on the rim of the telescope, trying to think what to do.

He opened his eyes and knew at once where he was. The light of the moon filled the whole of the rocket. It was so quiet, except for a strange humming sound that filled his ears. He caught a glimpse of the tiny clock and saw that it was half past eleven – there was only half an hour left until they got there. It was strange, but it seemed that the craft was just drifting through space now. He could hear no sound from the engines; it was as if they were a single tiny crystal floating through dark water. Toby forgot to be afraid. He stared about him, amazed and wondering. The humming that he'd heard when he woke up was the only sound there was. Suddenly he realised that it was like a strange song and he felt that it wasn't coming from the rocket at all. It seemed to come from space itself.

'Listen,' his uncle whispered.

'What is it?' Toby replied, hardly realising he was whispering himself.

'The song of the stars,' uncle Nichol told him.

Toby had never heard of such a thing. Was his uncle teasing him? He hadn't sounded much as if he was being funny.

'The song of the stars is what keeps everything in their perfect orbits,' he went on. 'It's been there since the very beginning of time. If we listened at night on earth we'd probably be able to hear it too, in some places at least. The problem is that we've so much noise now the song of the stars has been drowned out. All our cars and factories and talk have muffled it. But I think that I heard it, the time I was crossing the Atlantic.'

'Was that when you were struck by lightning?' Toby asked carefully.

His uncle nodded.

'But how did you find out about the song of the stars?' Toby asked.

Uncle Nichol moved about rather uncomfortably above him and didn't look at him. 'Oh, I must have read it somewhere, I suppose. Look at the moon, Daniel! Just look at it. And only another twenty minutes to go now.'

Every beat of the heart seemed to count now. Toby kept his eyes fixed on the surface of the moon. It was huge, all bright and silver, but filled with cracks and dents and valleys.

With every second that passed the rocket seemed to grow more full of its light. But Toby was thinking of his sum, that was all that mattered to him now. On earth it seemed simple enough working out the sums but now it all seemed so terribly huge. Their tiny rocket had to cross the path of the Little Moon at precisely the right moment. If it didn't the Little Moon would drift on on its four-year course and the rocket would be left heading towards the moon.

Neither of them could say a word. There was nothing that could be said. Both of them were just looking up at the face of the moon, watching. The only sound was that of the song of the stars and it drowned out everything else. The craft crept forwards like some black midge through the dark sea of space, closer and closer and closer. Just twelve minutes remained. The 29th of February was all but over.

'I think I see it,' uncle Nichol breathed. 'I wonder if you'll be able to from where you are, Daniel.'

Toby craned his neck to look. Out to the left and still far away he thought he could catch sight of something moving. It was unclear and sometimes he lost sight of it again, but after a minute he was pretty certain it was the thing uncle Nichol was meaning.

'Yes,' he breathed.

He scrabbled to find the telescope his uncle had given him for his birthday, the birthday that would soon be over. He remembered his dream of standing on the rim of the telescope counting the stars. It took him a moment to find it but he did at last. It winked as it moved; the great uneven surface seemed to reflect the moonlight and give off sudden sparks of brightness. It seemed so rugged, a mass of boulders and black debris. And with every second they were moving closer to it; there was nothing they could do to avoid it and all at once Toby realised just how fast they must still be moving, even though he hadn't heard the noise of the engines for such a time now.

'Six minutes to go,' his uncle breathed.

It was as though their heartbeats counted out the seconds.

The Little Moon now seemed to Toby to be like some great dark dragon moving towards them, its back covered with shimmering scales. He wasn't at all afraid any more; his heart was thumping for a different reason – in case they missed their target.

'When we get there, there'll be one terrible bang, Daniel,' uncle Nichol breathed. He sounded as if he meant it. A hundred other questions spun through Toby's head like falling stars but all of them melted away into dust as he kept his eyes on the Little Moon looming towards them. He didn't really want to watch at all and yet he couldn't help himself. Now the Little Moon looked like a black hedgehog spinning towards them. As the last minutes of his birthday passed so it came ever closer. He glanced at the clock above him – just four minutes left.

The moon's brightness was hurting his eyes now – it was hard to look towards it for any length of time. He had to turn back to the cabin of the rocket again for a moment and he saw that his hands were trembling.

'What will happen if we miss?' he asked out of the blue, but either uncle Nichol didn't hear him or else he didn't want to answer. He was just craning his neck all the time to watch the progress of the Little Moon; he didn't even stop to blink.

'Two minutes,' he murmured.

Toby began counting the seconds in his head. For a moment he remembered what it had been like at the other end, during the last minutes before take-off. None of this had seemed real then. It was more like a game of make-believe, an amazing adventure. For a moment he thought of his mum, of how she was. He thought of his dad, somewhere in a village near Glasgow. He thought about the snow at Alumbria, Tweedledum and Tweedledee, the bath at the top of the house, Mrs MacPherson. And that was his last thought, of Mrs MacPherson, as he looked down at the floor of the rocket and there was the most almighty roar, as he was flung over onto his side and the world went black.

11. The Rest of the Story

The first thing Toby remembered hearing was laughter. He thought he must be dreaming at first because he knew he had crashed in uncle Nichol's rocket and they were almost certain to be dead. It couldn't be laughter he was hearing. The only thing in front of his eyes was blackness, even when he opened them. He must be dead. But for a long time later he felt a pain in his left elbow and he thought that if he really was dead then he shouldn't feel any pain at all. And he was still hearing laughter. It was there at the back of his head, a bit like a fly buzzing on a windowpane, and it annoyed him – he wanted to swat it. Was he really dead? Was there laughter in heaven? And if he was in heaven then why was his arm hurting?

Then he heard his name being called, very softly and gently. The voice was still far away, but it was insistent, and it came back and back and back.

'Toby? Can you hear me? Toby?'

He didn't want to move. He was comfortable where he was and he liked having his eyes closed. He was tired and wanted nothing more than to go to sleep, right where he was.

'Toby! Speak to me! Are you all right, Toby?'

He opened his eyes again and forced himself up on his right arm. Perhaps he wasn't dead after all. The first thing he saw was a bar of chocolate. He didn't imagine there was chocolate in heaven.

'Yes,' he said slowly. 'I suppose I'm all right.'

The other person who'd been speaking had been his uncle. He recognised his voice now.

Toby remembered something. 'Why were you laughing?' he frowned. He massaged his sore elbow. He sat up and saw his uncle's face in front of his, but the wrong way up. His hair was spikier than ever.

'I was laughing because we'd made it!' uncle Nichol told him. 'There was part of me that didn't quite believe it would happen. I think we're all right. That means we might actually get home again! Now, ready to do some exploring?'

'Can't I sleep for a while?' Toby grumbled.

The face above him didn't smile any more.

'Come on, Daniel. You don't want me to go out there alone, do you? After all this? I brought you here to be part of it all. I need your help, I can't do it alone. You can sleep until the summer holidays once we get back. What d'you say, Daniel?'

Toby fumbled about and muttered something vaguely positive. His left arm was really hurting – he must have rolled over awkwardly when the rocket crashed into the Little Moon.

'Could you fish me out one or two things from the hold?' uncle Nichol asked him. Toby sighed and turned round awkwardly in the tight space. His eyes felt so terribly heavy.

'Now we need the water container and I'd like the small leather rucksack – careful of that. Well done, and there's a tiny telescope in the pocket of that jacket which I want with me. And we both need to wrap up now. It may feel warm in here, but I'm warning you. . . '

They scrabbled about with their overcoats for five minutes or more. It was so difficult to move about in that cramped space, but at least it helped to waken Toby. Even his arm felt a good bit better by the time he was finished.

Uncle Nichol looked down at him once more.

'Whatever we do, Toby, we must stay together, is that clear? The cold's going to hit us the moment we step outside, but we have to do everything we can to keep going. It'll be difficult to talk out there, so that means we have to stick close together to communicate in any way we can. Are you ready?'

The boy whose birthday had just ended nodded, a little doubtfully.

'Why don't we have the last bits of chocolate each?' his uncle suggested. 'Just to give us strength for when we get outside.'

Toby made his bit last. He felt frightened again, and he wasn't sure he wanted to do this. Everything seemed so big. . .

'Where are we going?' he asked, and his mouth felt like a dry cave.

'Just follow me and I'll tell you when we get there.'

His uncle opened the small door of the hatch and Toby heard the wind right away – he felt it too. It wasn't like anything he'd heard before and it ran shivers down his spine. Uncle Nichol looked up from the hatch. 'Good luck then, and whatever you do, don't give up. Trust me, Daniel. This is going to be the most special journey you ever made. And if anything should happen to me, I've written instructions on exactly what you'll have to do to get back home safely.'

Toby followed his uncle out onto the surface of the Little Moon. And the first thing he saw was the earth, and it took his breath away because it was so beautiful. This amazing blue ball, shining and spinning below him with its continents and oceans. One birthday he'd been given a globe by his mum that had a light inside it. He'd carried it up to bed and stood it on his bookcase in the corner of the room and put all the other lights out. He'd taken his finger and run it round the coasts of Africa and South America and Australia. Everything had seemed so big then. Even taking his finger round the coasts on the globe in his room had taken such a long time.

But now the strange thing was that the earth seemed small. It seemed like a toy. And what went through his head most of all was the thought that it was precious, wonderful and precious. It took his breath away. But then the wind caught him and almost blew him off his feet. He was knocked against the side of the rocket and his uncle reached out an arm to support him. He jerked his head to one side and they began walking out over the surface of the Little Moon, right into the teeth of the wind.

It was like walking across a silver lake. The rock beneath their feet was bathed in silver, and Toby couldn't tell if it was the earth's light or the moon's that made that strange and eerie pathway of light. He had to keep his head bent all the same – he could hardly look up to see what was ahead of him because of the power and the cruelty of that wind. It was the driest wind that Toby had ever felt; it was a wind made of the dust of stars. Those were the words that ran through his mind as he walked – *this wind is made of the dust of stars*. He felt there couldn't be so much as a drop of water in that place. All about their feet were the same black rocks – they rose up in jagged spars and their surfaces seemed to be covered with a strange glitter, a shining.

But the wind hurt. It hurt the face more than anything and it made his eyes run. That wind made him feel so dry; it made him feel as if his face had gone completely and had been replaced by a mask. Where were they going? How did his uncle know the way if he'd never really been there before? Had he been lying to Toby all along? Did he know what they were going to find and was it some terrible trap? A shadow of fear crossed his heart like dark wings. Yet his uncle had told him that it would be one of the most special journeys he'd ever make. He had to believe that was true.

They stopped together in the lee of some giant spars of rock, just to get their breath back. It was so good to be out of the wind; Toby crouched down and tiredness came over him at once. If only he could sleep. . .

But his uncle must have noticed because he began hauling him to his feet. Toby winced; his wail of protest was blown away by the wind. But all at once he saw something, a strange metal shape half-buried in the black dust. It looked like an eagle. . .

He pulled away from his uncle and reached out with his hand to grasp the thing. It was so heavy, for a second he wasn't sure he could lift it at all. But he got a proper hold of it in the end and held it up in front of his uncle. To his great surprise he saw him nodding, nodding and smiling. He'd been sure he would be amazed, amazed and curious, but it was as if he'd always known the eagle was there, just waiting to be found. He bent down and shouted something to Toby, but the words were blown away like dust and Toby didn't catch so much as a syllable. Then his uncle took the eagle and laid it carefully back on the ground between the jagged black rocks. He motioned for Toby to follow him.

The next minutes seemed to last forever. They didn't even feel like minutes but rather hours. On and on they plodded over that uneven ground until Toby's feet hurt with the pain of the sharp stones he'd crossed. But it was relentless, a dry wind that ate your fingers to the bone and blew your face to white pain.

In the end Toby felt he couldn't have spoken even if he'd wanted to. Nor could he have held the eagle if he'd still been carrying it. All he did was let one foot trail after another behind his uncle. Sometimes he felt so tired and hopeless he'd have given up altogether and gone to lie down in the shelter of the great black rocks.

Sometimes he wanted to cry but it felt as if even his tears had been blown to dry grains of sand at the back of his eyes. Where was it they were going? What on earth was the point? Were they going all the way round the Little Moon? There were times he found his uncle hard to bear. He walked behind him and looked up at the silly spikes of white hair sticking straight up into the air. He looked mad and Toby thought that was exactly what he was. Mad and selfish and thoughtless.

Then the pain of the wind would come back again and he wondered if it would be possible to slip away after all and rest. If his uncle wanted to walk another ten miles that was up to him – he wasn't going to find anything, but if that was really what he wanted to do then fair enough. But Toby couldn't. He'd promised. And somehow or other he had to believe his uncle when he said this journey was going to be special. He found it almost impossible but he had to believe.

Toby lost all sense of time. But what seemed like hours after they'd started out from the rocket he thought he saw something ahead. It was still so far off it was difficult to be certain, but he was pretty sure all the same. Something dark, something that rose up from the surface of the Little Moon and was different. Perhaps it was nothing more than the same black spars of rock they'd passed; perhaps he was imagining things because he was so desperate for this to be over at last. Yet as they struggled closer against the wind and the dust he grew more sure all the time.

He began to count his steps. It was the only thing he could do to keep going. He was afraid that otherwise he might just topple over eventually and not get up again at all. He didn't even have the strength any more to look up to see where the black shadow ahead of them was. He bent his head and he counted his steps as his feet passed over the uneven ground. One hundred and eighty-six, one hundred and eighty seven, one hundred and eighty eight. . .

Uncle Nichol was a good way ahead of him, but it didn't matter. All that mattered to Toby now was reaching safety and resting. It felt as if he was trapped in a strange and terrible dream he had to waken from before it was too late.

He glanced up and saw that his uncle had disappeared from view. There was dust swirling about in the fierce wind, and hard edges of stone stung the boy's eyes so the tears ran. There was something ahead of him, something that loomed up from the ground. Where had his uncle gone? Toby reached out with his arms, searching blindly for something to hold onto. He staggered forwards another couple of feet and his hands did strike something that felt like a rock wall.

Toby felt his way round it with careful fingers; he managed to open his eyes just and no more and see the black stone towering above him. This must have been what he'd seen from far away; this must have been what uncle Nichol was making for all the time. But where had he gone? Was it some kind of trap? Had he disappeared? Toby felt his throat tighten with fear. What if he did have to get back alone, without his uncle? How in the world would he ever manage it?

He shouted his name, more in fear than anything else, but his voice was snatched away from him by the wind. It was no use. All of a sudden he felt strong arms pulling him down and he half staggered forwards into what felt like empty darkness. He banged one arm against rock as he reached out to try to break his fall. But suddenly there was silence. It was the most extraordinary thing in the world. He could still hear the wind, but far away now, and he opened his eyes. It was pitch dark. Then suddenly there was the sound of a match being struck and he saw uncle Nichol's face in front of his own, his chin and cheeks all lit up golden by candlelight.

He could hear again. He could hear his heart. They were in some kind of cavern. It echoed when he moved his feet.

'Well done, Daniel,' his uncle said.

'Where are we?' Toby said, looking straight at him.

'You knew all along we were coming here and you never said a word back at the rocket! What is it you're not telling me?'

His uncle's eyes swivelled sheepishly and he licked his lips. 'All right, I'm sorry I haven't told you everything, but it was never for any bad reason. I promise you that. Come deeper into the cave and I'll explain. It's wide enough for us to walk together.'

Toby did as he was told – he didn't have any choice. His uncle was right – the cave was wider, but it was very low, so that walking forward meant you had to be almost hunched double. They seemed to be going downwards, and Toby wasn't sure he felt all that happy. It was getting warmer with every second that passed and he felt shut in. They were right inside the Little Moon.

But then he heard another sound. It was strange to his ears at first, like nothing he had ever heard before. Then gradually it seemed to become familiar but he couldn't quite put his finger on what it was. It was very like something he knew and he was racking his brains to remember what. But the warmth of the cave made him even sleepier than before; the absence of that freezing wind left him tired and much less ready to fight. The further they went along the passage the more his eyelids started to droop.

Then, all at once, he knew what it was – the sound of water! But could it be? The Little Moon seemed the last place ever where there would be water. The rocks they had struggled through after leaving the rocket had been as dry as dust. Yet it sounded more and more like running water the closer they went.

All at once the passage opened up into a much larger cave, almost like a bell. Suddenly it was possible for both Toby and his uncle to stand tall again, and in the candlelight the boy saw a silver spray of water rippling upwards from the stone floor. It was like magic. But what Toby noticed even more was a strange golden shining all round the little spring of water. At first he thought it was because of his uncle's candle but then he saw that it was only just where the ground shone gold. His uncle had stopped and was smiling, smiling and nodding, as if he had been right about something all along.

'What is it?' Toby cried. 'Tell me!'

His uncle looked at him. For a second he did no more than just look at him and his eyes were shining. He looked at Toby and he didn't say a single word. Then he glanced away and brought out a tightly crumpled ball of paper. Very carefully he unravelled it.

'D'you remember the book, Daniel? The one from Luxor?'

Of course Toby remembered.

'There *was* more to the story, more that I translated. I didn't want to tell you all of it before we got here, because I wasn't even sure we would make it. You mustn't blame me, Daniel. But now I can read it, now that we're really here:

'It was while he was there he discovered a handful of dust that was to change his life for ever. The Little Moon is composed of dark stone. It is a terrible place where storms rage continuously and dust fills the air. Even to walk a step there takes courage. But he did not flinch from the struggle, and fought against the wind for many hours until he came to a place of sanctuary. The mountains of the Little Moon are not as ours, yet the black stone stretches many cubits into the sky, and inside its walls is a labyrinth of caves. He walked a good way inside, and came to a place where water sprang up from the stone floor in a magical spout. He said that water tasted like no water he had ever drunk on earth, it satisfied him as water never had before. And around about was a strange golden dust that gave off a light all of its own – he called it – star dust. It was this he had brought back with him from the Little Moon, this star dust, and with it he had healed many wounds. And I begged him for but one grain, for my son had suffered a dreadful illness since childhood, and no doctor could make him well.

Imagine my joy. . .'

'That is where the passage ends,' uncle Nichol whispered, folding up the piece of paper with reverence. He bent down gently towards the spring, very carefully, almost as if he was afraid he would disturb the water. He cupped his hands about the liquid and drank deeply, and he closed his eyes as he did so. Toby felt thirsty as he watched him, almost envious, but he kept standing just where he was and didn't move a muscle.

Then uncle Nichol moved back from the spring. He put out one cupped hand towards the gold dust and Toby saw that his hand was trembling. He moved it millimetre by millimetre until he touched it at last. Then he lifted it with his fingers and let it trickle back among the stones. As Toby watched it the dust became like a single golden stream. In all his life Toby had never seen anything so bright. His uncle looked up at him and smiled.

'Star dust,' he breathed. 'That's why I came here, Daniel.'

He brought out a tiny silver box with a lid. Then all at once he remembered something. 'Do you remember the eagle, the stone eagle we found when we left the rocket?'

Toby nodded, 'That was from the Roman rocket, wasn't

it? That was the first flight, when they came here and found this place!'

His uncle just looked at him and nodded, his eyes bright. 'That was the first flight.' He turned away and with trembling hands he reached out towards the star dust.

All at once Toby understood. He had a clear picture of his mother in the hospital bed in Edinburgh. She looked so pale and yet so beautiful it made his eyes burn with love. He could see everything so clearly – the apples and pears on the white stand beside her bed, the window that was just a few centimetres open. Somehow he knew that it was the middle of the night there too; he really felt that somehow or other he was looking through a strange window, back onto the real world and his mother's room.

Suddenly he saw that his uncle was looking at him again.

'I want you to take some too,' he whispered. 'I want you to take some star dust, Daniel.'

'Why?'

'In case anything happens to me. This is the one chance we have.'

He spoke those words so quietly they were soft as dust themselves, they were barely more than a breath. But Toby heard them just the same. He understood. He got up and went over to join his uncle.

'Try the water, Daniel. Just taste it.'

He did. The cold of it against his fingers was like an electric shock. He almost jumped backwards when he felt it. He brought his dripping hands up to his mouth and drank. He felt it burning icily all the way to his tummy but it was wonderful just the same. Somehow he felt so pure after he'd drunk it, so pure and peaceful. It seemed to be more than just water. It was strange too that he didn't need to dry his hands on his coat afterwards – already his palms were completely dry.

But where was he to keep the star dust? He couldn't think until suddenly he realised he was still holding the little telescope in one hand. His uncle had given him a soft pouch in which to carry it, a pouch made of red velvet. He glanced at his uncle as he held it in his hand, as if to ask if it would be all right. Uncle Nichol closed his eyes and nodded. Toby bent down and took up a little handful of the star dust. Every grain was like a single diamond, and even that tiny handful seemed heavy between his fingers. He let the little trail of dust fall into the pouch and he was almost sure he could hear the grains as they landed. Not one remained on his fingers.

'All right then,' his uncle said. 'Are you ready to go home?' Toby nodded.

Uncle Nichol put his hand on his. 'Thank you for having the courage you've shown, Daniel. I'm proud of you. I told you I couldn't do this on my own and I meant it. D'you know why I called you Daniel, all those years ago, about the time you had your first real birthday, on the 29th of February when you were four?'

Toby shook his head.

'Because of Daniel and the lions' den. Daniel had the courage to go into that den with the lions, not be afraid of getting killed.'

'I'm not all that brave,' Toby breathed, and he had to fight hard not to cry. 'I'm not brave when Billy Cartwright calls me names and I'm not all that brave when I have to jump from the diving board in swimming.'

Uncle Nichol squeezed his hand. 'That's not the kind of bravery I'm talking about. I'm talking about having the courage to be your own person, to be different. It's much easier to be a Billy Cartwright than a Toby Goodwin. It's much easier to be one of the crowd than to be different. But it's the different people who count. They're the ones who're remembered. And if the world didn't have them, then there'd be no point going on. D'you see what I mean?'

Toby wasn't sure but he thought so. His uncle ruffled his hair and got up.

'Come on, let's go back and make a difference,' he said.

12. The Storm

They were almost blown back to the rocket. The great wind they had fought against with all their might to reach the caves was behind them now. Toby had hidden the little red pouch full of star dust deep inside his clothing, making sure it was tied securely so that not a single speck would be lost. He didn't feel tired any longer; he realised that it must be three or four in the morning now – later than he'd ever stayed up before – but he didn't feel tired all the same. Somehow he was beyond being tired.

He walked behind his uncle this time too, but now it was so that he wouldn't be blown away by the force of the silver wind at his back. It came in such terrible gusts, and sometimes he imagined there were voices in it, strange ghostly voices that might almost have been from long, long ago. He walked right behind his uncle, his head down, one step after another. Suddenly he realised how glad he was not to be alone here – it would have terrified him to feel this huge dark emptiness of space on his own.

All of a sudden his uncle stopped in his tracks. For a brief second Toby thought they must be there, back at the rocket, and his heart leapt for joy. But then he looked up and saw nothing but the same empty expanse of dust and stone ahead, and his shoulders slumped.

'Daniel!' uncle Nichol shouted against the weird howling

of the wind. 'Can you see anything? Anything to show the way back?

He looked. He stood there alongside his uncle, swaying as the wind whirled and fumed about him like some mighty wild animal. Perhaps it was the most frightening moment of his life. They had had a landmark to make for on the journey from the rocket; they had seen the high rocks and the caves. But now there was nothing at all – every bit of ground was the same.

A horrible thought crossed Toby's mind – perhaps they'd passed the rocket already, perhaps they hadn't seen it in time or already it had been hidden under a layer of dust so it looked no different to the other looming boulders on the Little Moon.

At that moment he felt tired, so desperately tired. He had hoped they might be back already when uncle Nichol stopped in his tracks, and instead they were as far away as ever. Except they did not know how far away they were because they were lost. How long could they survive out here on the storm-bound surface of the Little Moon, trudging on in circles, growing more and more exhausted all the time?

His uncle put his hands on his shoulders, shielded him from another great gust of wind. Toby forced himself to look one more time, to let his eyes range round ahead of them to try to find something, anything that might point the way back. And suddenly he did see something after all. It was a tiny piece of silver about ten metres ahead of them, and he had spotted it because it was shining so brightly, almost like the beam of a torch. But even from there Toby was sure he knew what it was. He pointed in triumph.

'Look! The eagle!'

It was the eagle from the Roman rocket, the one that had lain not far from where they themselves landed. The two of them began battling away over the last ground as fast as they could move, thrilled and full of relief.

When they came to it, Toby bent down and picked it up triumphantly with both hands. This was going to come back with him. But all at once he felt the touch of his uncle's hand again his arm; he was shaking his head and motioning for Toby to put it back down. Reluctantly Toby did, not understanding.

Then uncle Nichol produced the flag he had brought from home, the Randolph flag. It was attached to a short, stout stick and he squatted down, drove it with all his might into the hard, dry ground of the Little Moon. It was right beside the eagle. The flag fluttered madly in the terrible wind that tore across the surface of the Little Moon – it waved in spite of the fury of the storm. Toby thought he understood all the same. The eagle was all that survived of the rocket that had come those centuries ago, and in a way the Randolph flag was all that would remain of their rocket. Toby looked at the flag and realised that one day it would be gone completely, the last threads would blow away and the stick would disappear into the ground. That was the frightening thing about time, it took everything away in the end. All that would remain would be the little metal hook that attached the flag to the stick. He shivered, because he was cold and because he was frightened. Time was too big to think about.

Uncle Nichol and he went the last bit of the way to the rocket. There was a layer of dust on it already, and as he stood there looking at it, waiting for his uncle to open the hatch, he realised that it looked as it had been there for hundreds or even thousands of years. It looked as if it was made of the very rock of the Little Moon, or as if it was a single fossil. Then uncle Nichol managed to open the hatch and the two of them slipped inside on their hands and knees.

For a second they just crouched there listening to the howling of the wind. It was the emptiest sound Toby had ever heard in his life and he felt so glad to be back there safely. Soon they would be back home again and the first person he would find would be his mother.

'I have something to tell you, Toby.'

He looked round sharply towards his uncle. There was a difference in his voice that worried him, and the fact that he used his real name.

He frowned at his uncle, not understanding. He was as white as a ghost.

'I don't know how to get home,' he whispered.

'What d'you mean?'

His uncle seemed almost unable to look at him. 'I knew how to get here, Toby. The manuscript told me that. But it said almost nothing about getting back.' He swallowed and looked at his nephew in fear. 'I'm not sure how to steer. We came down heavily when we landed, you remember? I'm not sure if the engines will even have survived.' He paused, looked away for a moment and then turned back towards Toby. His eyes were big and full of pain, and that was the thing which made Toby most frightened of all. It wasn't so much the danger of the situation, it was the fact that uncle Nichol was afraid. At that moment he wanted to shake his uncle and shout at him. He wanted to ask him a hundred questions, about why he hadn't said a thing before they left, about how he could have risked their lives in this way. But he knew none of that would help, and he also knew that this was exactly what his mother always said uncle Nichol was like. He was very good at starting things, but very bad at finishing them. He listened and he heard the wind shaking the rocket as if it was made of paper. How were they ever to get home now?

'Was there anything at all?' he asked at last. 'Was there any clue in the story?'

Uncle Nichol looked down, covered his mouth with his hand, thinking hard. He looked up sharply. 'Only one thing, one phrase. It said that the ship came down like a ghost. Yes, those were the words – *the ship came down like a ghost*. But it means nothing, it means nothing at all. That's just poetry.'

For a second his nephew just looked at him. A moment before Toby had believed it was just a matter of time before they would be back at home and on his way to find his mother. Suddenly everything had changed. What if they never got home? A terrible cold hand of fear ran up Toby's spine and over his neck. He felt his heart thumping in his chest and very quickly his mouth turned dry as a desert. He couldn't speak – it was hard enough to think. He kept on thinking about those words – the ship came down like a ghost. Then suddenly something came to him.

'I don't think it is just poetry. I think it's really telling us something.'

His uncle looked at him, his head on one side. There was something in the eagerness of Toby's voice that made him listen, want to hear more.

Toby sat up and leant closer. 'I think it means the engines weren't used at all! I think it means the ship just fell back to earth, allowed itself to be carried! If it was steered properly, that would be possible!' He was excited now, he could hear his heart racing. 'All we need to work out is our direction, and leave at exactly the right moment. Just like we did to come here. I have to go outside first!'

'Be careful!' his uncle said, and gripped his arm as he crawled past and went back into the Little Moon's storm. For a second his eyes were blinded with dust. He crawled to his feet at last and was almost blown away by the strength of the wind. His eyes searched behind him. There was the earth, like a huge blue ball in the sky. It was so beautiful, so amazing. For a second it was hard to believe that that was where he came from, that somewhere on that globe was Edinburgh and home and his mum. Perhaps she was looking out of her window in hospital right at that very same time.

Then he forced himself to think. He had to work it out. He had to know the timing. There was America, he recognised the shape of North and South America at once. It was turning away, slowly turning into the shadows. . .

He crawled back inside. His uncle said nothing, just handed him a whole sheaf of figures of distances and times and locations. For a second Toby's eyes blurred and he could see none of them. His uncle was telling him a hundred different things but he couldn't hear a thing; the words didn't make any sense. He realised he was holding a pencil between his fingers and he wasn't even sure how it got there. He forced himself to concentrate, to focus on the wind that howled round them on the surface of the Little Moon. He had to be brave.

All at once he remembered a time when Billy Cartwright had come into the classroom at lunchtime with three of the other bullies. Toby had been sitting in a seat where he couldn't be seen from the door. He was there on his own doing maths homework because he knew there wouldn't be time that evening. He was the only one in the classroom. If Billy Cartwright found him there who knew what would happen? But they hadn't seen him yet; they were standing laughing by the door. He had to force himself to go on with his maths, to concentrate. The worst thing would be to let them know he was there. He put his head down on the desk and forced himself to think about nothing else but the next sum. And apart from Billy Cartwright's voice the only thing he could hear was the wind gusting over the school playground. . .

He had to find the starting point, the first bit of the sum. That was what his first maths teacher had always told him and he tried never to forget that. The problem was that his uncle had scribbled so many figures down in panic it was hard to understand how one was linked to another. What if he couldn't do it? What if, for the first time in his life, he didn't know how to find the answer? Then he saw his mum in his mind's eye, just as he had done when they crouched in the strange caves before returning with star dust. This was why he had to find the answer; it was for her sake. And there it was, the starting point. He saw a possible chain. That trembling began in his hands which he always got when he was working. It was like that blue curl of fire that creeps along a piece of paper when a fire's being lit. All of a sudden it grows into orange light and the first flames appear.

'How are you getting on, Toby?' his uncle asked, and there was worry in his voice.

'Give me another five minutes.' Toby replied, but there was the tiniest edge of a smile on his lips.

Uncle Nichol sat beside the hatch window, looking out on the Little Moon. He had waited for this moment for so long, and now that it had come he was utterly afraid. Thoughts went through his head like a storm, but he didn't say a single word.

'I think I've got it,' Toby said softly. He was looking up, his face very pale but his eyes shining.

'I think I know when we have to leave and what our course should be. We have just another twenty minutes.'

'Twenty minutes! Then help me, boy! We haven't a moment to lose!'

They had to make the craft ready for the return journey. They had to clear the worst of the debris that had blown over the rocket, make sure that everything was clear. The wind howled about Toby as his hands swept back and forth across the buried panels, and he had to close his eyes so the dust wouldn't blind him. His uncle shouted something at the top of his voice but the words were ripped away by the wind. Toby staggered back to the hatch and fumbled his way inside; his fingers felt raw and numb.

'It's a storm,' his uncle said, getting his breath back as best he could. 'The timing couldn't be worse. We've got just twelve minutes left. If only the engines. . .'

They sat there together for the next minutes, unable to do another thing, as the storm raged about them on the Little Moon and everything outside became a blinding whirl of grey dust. The only words in Toby's head were thirty-seven, that was the angle of the course they had to steer back to earth. Thirty-seven, thirty-seven, thirty-seven – the words thumped like a strange heartbeat in his head.

'Are you ready?' uncle Nichol whispered from where he was sitting at the top of the rocket. He looked down at Toby in the shadows and all his nephew could see were the whites of his eyes. Toby didn't say a word, he just nodded.

Ten, nine, eight, seven, six. . . .It seemed to Toby that just at the critical moment the wind lessened, there was a lull. He hardly noticed that he was holding his breath, not daring even to breathe. . . Five, four, three, two, one – he didn't let out his breath but just listened, strained his ears for any sound that wasn't that of the raging wind. And there, he was sure, it was climbing and growing so that the sides of the rocket were trembling with life. The engines had started. Uncle Nichol glanced down once more, just for the tiniest of seconds, and they exchanged a glimmer of a smile, no words. But it was enough to express everything.

The rocket rose into the air and Toby caught a last glimpse of the Little Moon before they climbed away from it for ever and it spun away from them, continuing its strange and secret journey.

'I'll look for you, I promise,' Toby whispered to himself. 'Every time my real birthday comes back I'll look for you.'

'What did you work out our course to be?' uncle Nichol asked, and his voice was quieter now and calmer.

'Thirty-seven degrees,' Toby answered, 'and now you can turn off the engines, let us glide back. You can let the ship come down like a ghost.' The words had sounded so strange and frightening on the Little Moon, now somehow they seemed beautiful to him. It was only now they meant something, it was only now they counted. And what they meant first and foremost was home.

'Thirty-seven,' uncle Nichol repeated with admiration. 'Thirty-seven. You see, I was right, Toby. I told you I needed you – I told you I couldn't do this without you.'

Toby nodded. He didn't say anything, and uncle Nichol couldn't see him, but he nodded all the same. He thought of all the times he'd sat in his Edinburgh classroom doing maths, not really understanding what the point was. He loved doing the sums and he never failed to find the right answer, but so often he wondered what the point was, what the purpose behind the sum was. Now he knew, now he understood. The answer thirty-seven meant the journey back to earth, it meant home, it meant everything.

'Soon we'll just be falling at that course,' his uncle said, not looking at him but lifting a red lever Toby hadn't noticed before, very gradually and carefully.

'We'll fall back to Scotland as soft as thistledown. We'll be home by early morning, Toby, so if you want to catch some sleep you can. It's been a long birthday. The longest I imagine you'll ever have.'

Toby still didn't say anything. He didn't know what he felt because he felt so many things all at the one time. Tired and content and hungry and confused and happy all at once – it was as if there wasn't more room in his head for all the different things he felt. But that didn't seem bad all the same. It actually felt good. He touched the pouch that held his handful of star dust and he smiled.

All of a sudden he caught sight of the earth, through one of the tiny side windows in the rocket. He almost gasped with the thrill of that sight. It was the most amazing thing there could be. The sky that surrounded it was utterly black, totally and completely dark. But the seas looked so blue, so clear and pure and blue. It was hard to believe they could be that blue after all that had been done to them, but they were. Toby closed his right eye and took his little finger and drew it in a circle round the globe. No-one had ever been faster round the world than he had – he was breaking record after record by the second.

'Now we're just falling,' uncle Nichol said quietly, and it was as if Toby suddenly woke up. He didn't look at his uncle, he just listened instead to the silence. That was the thing he was most conscious of – the huge silence. When they'd set off for the Little Moon there had been nothing but the roaring of the engines and the great trembling of the rocket – now there was nothing but the hugeness of the silence. They were falling like a single snowflake onto the world, drifting out of space to touch down on earth again as soft as a kiss. Toby felt a great lightness inside, and a strong sensation of falling. But he couldn't decide if he felt very, very heavy or very, very light. He was still thinking about that and arguing with himself in his own head when he must have fallen asleep. He dreamed that he was back on earth and that it was autumn. Somehow or other he knew that he had to go into hibernation, and he rolled up in a deep pile of leaves like a hedgehog. It smelled wonderful in there, of acorns and earth and wood smoke. It was beautifully quiet and he knew he was going to sleep there all through the autumn until spring came back once more. . .

'Toby, are you awake? We've just another hour to go.'

He opened his eyes slowly, without any sense of panic or surprise. He knew exactly where he was. Gone were the last of his feelings of fear. He looked out of the tiny hatch window and realised he was now seeing just one corner of the earth, half-shrouded in cloud. It was like looking at the edge of someone's eyeball from very close up.

'What are you going to do now?' Toby asked suddenly, without even really thinking about the question.

'What am I going to do?' uncle Nichol replied, squinting down to look at his nephew. He gave a half laugh and his eyes twinkled, but somehow Toby knew that he was surprised by the question, that he really didn't know what to say. He was always the one who gave the questions, but he didn't really like getting them himself.

'I'm going to go home and put my feet up,' he said loudly, not looking at Toby at all but busying himself with the dials.

'But after that,' Toby persisted. 'Once you've recovered and got everything back to normal, what then?'

Toby asked because he suddenly realised that so much of his uncle's life had been poured into this quest, this journey to the Little Moon. Now he'd managed it; now he'd come back. It was a bit like Christopher Columbus coming home from America – how was it possible to go back to everyday life? How could you begin all over again and be happy? After all that had gone before? His uncle's face looked down at his own, grey and sad and rather old looking. It looked rather like a moon itself, a lined silver old moon hanging on its own lonely sky.

'Maybe I'll write a book,' he murmured, and Toby nodded. 'And I'd like to spend more time with your mum,' he went on, his voice even quieter.

'I'd like to come a lot more to Alumbria,' Toby said. 'Would that be all right, uncle Nichol?'

His uncle kept looking down at him and his eyes seemed to go a bit funny. He didn't say anything. He just nodded and nodded.

The earth was coming closer and closer. It hardly seemed any time since Toby had been looking at it from the Little Moon and drawing it with his finger. Then it had seemed so tiny, no larger than a blue ball on a Christmas tree. Now it was so big he could barely see its edge any more; they were falling down towards it all the time and it was growing to fill the whole sky. Already the Little Moon seemed like a distant dream.

Suddenly he began to wonder just how accurate his maths had been. It was impossible to work out what the wind would do; it was still possible that it might blow them off course. Imagine if they landed right in the middle of London! Or in the North Sea! Perhaps they might come down in France – at once Toby began going over in his head the few bits of French he knew.

Somehow he could tell they were coming close to the ground; he didn't know quite why but he was sure he could feel it. There was a sort of lightness in his tummy and he closed his eyes, afraid there might be the kind of crash there was when they landed on the Little Moon. He thought he heard uncle Nichol saying something, but he couldn't hear a thing because his ears had gone all funny. Then there was a loud bang and he didn't know which way up he was. He felt strange and dizzy. Then he opened his eyes and listened and realised they were home. He saw his uncle looking at him from somewhere different altogether.

'We'd better see where we are then,' he said, and disappeared. The first thing Toby realised when the hatch door was opened was just how very cold it was. The second thing that crossed his mind was that it was the first of March. Then he crawled out of the tiny hatch and realised that his face was in something long and green and sticky. They were in a field and his uncle had just stood in something unmentionable. He said something that was even less mentionable. Toby giggled.

A dog was barking somewhere, and in a building away over to their left lights had come on. All at once he felt uncle Nichol's hand on his arm.

'Hush, Toby, not a sound now. The last thing we want is for them to find the rocket.'

Toby didn't even nod in case that made too much noise. He kept still as a post, his eyes fixed on the distant farmhouse.

He wanted to shiver because he was cold, but he managed to suppress even that. The two of them seemed to stand there like that for an eternity. Toby wasn't even sure he could manage it much longer; his legs were aching and he was so cold he couldn't feel the ends of his fingers. Then, to his relief, he saw the ground floor lights of the building going off again. Uncle Nichol seemed to breathe a great sigh of relief.

'How far away are we?'

'From where?' his uncle asked sharply. 'You mean from Alumbria?'

Toby nodded in the dark. 'Yes,' he breathed.

There was quiet for a while longer. Uncle Nichol was looking all round, very slowly. He almost looked like a ghost in the dark, his long white hair sticking out at weird angles from his pale face. For a second Toby was tempted to giggle.

Just then there was a noise, very far away. Uncle Nichol's head spun round in the direction it seemed to be coming from. 'Hush!' he said loudly, even though Toby hadn't said a word. He was listening, his head on one side and his eyes wide and staring. Now Toby thought he looked like a barn owl. But slowly a smile spread over his uncle's face.

'D'you know what that was?' he asked, his voice a bit louder. Toby just shook his head. He wasn't sure he'd heard anything at all. The only sound had been his own teeth chattering. All at once a church bell rang out, five slow times.

'I'm sure that's the village bell,' uncle Nichol breathed, his head tilted on one side. Then there was another noise, a muffled barking. 'I'll tell you what that was. It was Tweedledee,' uncle Nichol said with satisfaction. 'I would know that bark a hundred miles away. He was smelling a rat near the house.'

He turned to look at Toby, a smile stretching from ear to ear. 'We're less than twenty minutes from Alumbria, Toby. That's how close you got us to home. We almost landed in the garden.' He ruffled his nephew's hair and Toby blushed. He was glad his uncle wouldn't see his red face in the dark. But he felt a wonderful glow inside all the same – he was so happy. It was the best sum he had ever done in his whole life.

All at once his uncle pulled him unexpectedly away.

'Come back into the rocket for a minute, Toby. We have to be as quick as we possibly can.'

Toby didn't say a thing, obediently followed his uncle into the shelter of the rocket. Had his uncle seen something? Had they been found? But uncle Nichol switched on a tiny light in the rocket, and surely if they had been spotted that was the last thing he would do. He pulled out a piece of paper, the scrap on which the Latin words about the Little Moon had been written. He turned it over, laid it on a smooth surface, and found a pen. Finally he looked intently at his nephew, his grey eyes glittering.

'We have to get you to Edinburgh as quickly as possible, Toby. We didn't go to the Little Moon for nothing, you know. I want you to reach your mother by dawn – there isn't a moment to lose. Now look here. I know the field we've landed in – I'm not quite sure how far the railway is from here, but I reckon it's about ten minutes. There'll be a goods train passing at a quarter past five, going into the city. We have to catch it. Or rather, you have to catch it. Are you ready to run?'

Toby wasn't sure what to say; he felt too bewildered.

'What about the rocket?' he breathed.

His uncle looked at him, frustrated. 'Don't worry about

that!' he said. He shrugged his shoulders. 'It doesn't matter now, Toby! I've done what I set out to do and that's the important thing! All that matters is getting you to Edinburgh. Are you ready?'

Toby waited one last moment, not quite believing, and then he realised he had no choice but to nod. He would never have believed that his uncle could run so fast. His mother had once told him that Nichol Randolph had been chased by an angry bull when he was twelve years old. Then he had been the fastest thing on two legs, but that was an awfully long time ago. Yet even though his hair had turned white, his legs certainly hadn't grown any slower. Toby had a job to keep up with him at all. It was as if he could smell the train coming. He set off across the field at an angle like a rabbit being chased by a terrier. He seemed to know the exact way to go. Suddenly they were at the edge of the field and uncle Nichol was clambering over a fence into some trees. Then they were rushing up a steep slope, and by now Toby was completely out of breath. His heart was in his mouth and he felt dizzy and bewildered; a branch had scratched his cheek and he was sure his trousers had been torn. Those things didn't really matter, but he wasn't at all sure he could go on running for much longer. The slope seemed to go on for ever and he slipped in the deep pile of autumn leaves that buried his ankles. His uncle shouted something to encourage him, but Toby couldn't hear any of the words. He just felt himself being hauled to his feet and at last they were at the top and out into another bit of field. Now his uncle was ahead of him and getting further away all the time. His white hair shone out in the dark like an exploding star.

'Not far now, Toby! You can almost see the station!'

Toby hoped and prayed that his uncle was right. There was nothing worse than someone promising you were nearly there, and 'there' getting further and further away all the time. But he had to believe now, he had to keep going.

He thought of Billy Cartwright then and his heart nearly failed him. He remembered doing a cross country run one autumn and they tripped him up so that he fell flat on his face in a pool of muddy water.

'Milk chocolate!' Billy Cartwright shrieked, and all the others roared with laughter. He had been the last one to get back to school, his shoes still filled with brown water.

But the strange thing was that now it was different, even though he didn't quite understand why. Maybe it was because the memory made him feel angry. He clenched his fists and pounded over the dark ground, hardly remembering that he couldn't see the way ahead. He began to catch up on his uncle, and very far away he was almost certain he could see the station, just as his uncle had promised.

13. The Train

Toby caught up with his uncle and they shared a second's glance. But he saw that Uncle Nichol looked suddenly exhausted, almost as if he had grown ten years older in the time since he left the rocket. His face was so white and all filled with lines – he didn't look as if he would make it.

'Come on, uncle Nichol!' he cried, and smiled. It was a smile of hope, of triumph, of belief. His uncle didn't smile back but he'd been given something all the same to keep him going. There wasn't far to go; soon they would be out onto the station platform.

It seemed so strange to Toby to be back there now. It felt as if weeks and weeks had passed since he'd arrived there, since he was going to face the worst days of his life. It was only a few days ago and it seemed impossible to believe. This time the station was all shut up and there was no manager in sight. The place was deserted – it was twelve minutes past five. Toby forced himself to breathe more easily – he held his breath and listened. Very far away he was sure he could hear something, the sound of an engine. The goods train was coming; it was on time. Toby whirled round to see where his uncle was; he was hobbling along, his head down, looking for all the world as if his next step would be his last. Toby went to catch hold of him before he fell – uncle Nichol clutched his hand in his own as he did so.

'I'll be all right, Daniel.'

It was no more than a whisper, but there was a glint of a smile in his eyes all the same. Toby knew he would be all right. The noise of the engine was getting louder all the time.

'I was right to give you that name, and you've earned it now.'

'What d'you mean?'

His uncle looked up at him, still fighting to catch his breath. His hair looked like a haystack that had had an electric shock. And uncle Nichol had been struck by lightning – twice.

'Daniel and the lions' den. Daniel was afraid but he didn't run away, he faced the danger and won through in the end. Just what you've done. I called you Daniel because I always wanted you to be brave, to be strong and full of courage. When you were little you were frightened of everything, you were forever crying. Now you've shown real courage; you've faced the lions. That's something the bullies won't ever take away from you, and don't you forget it.'

The last words were almost lost because of the noise of the approaching train. It was coming round the far corner, sparks chasing from its wheels like fireflies. Out of the corner of his eye Toby saw his uncle whirling his arms about, jumping up and down in order to catch the attention of the driver, to get him to stop. Toby did the same. They shouted, they waved, they swayed about on the platform like a couple of madmen. Toby caught a moment's glimpse of the driver; he was wearing round glasses and had a beard. His face was startled – he looked as if he'd seen a ghost.

Certainly anyone was going to be fairly taken aback by uncle Nichol dancing about like a dervish on a station platform at five fifteen in the morning, his hair sticking up like icicles all over his head. The driver jammed on his brakes and the air was filled with the most awful squealing Toby had ever heard in his life. Uncle Nichol was babbling something to him but he couldn't hear a word. He found himself running back down the platform – the goods train had come to a standstill ten or twenty metres down the track. The man with the beard and glasses was looking back at them from his engines.

'You'd better have stopped me for something serious,' he warned them. 'If you're going to tell me you want a ticket to Bournemouth then you won't get much sympathy.'

Uncle Nichol reached him first. 'If you might be so kind as to take this young gentleman as close as you can to Edinburgh you may well be saving a life. Not his but someone else's.'

The driver didn't say anything for a moment, but his eyes flickered from uncle Nichol to Toby and back again. He scratched his left eyebrow and frowned.

'By rights I'd be breaking the law,' he said doubtfully, 'and if I get caught I might never drive another train. . . '

'But this is one time in a million,' uncle Nichol said, his voice quieter and more serious than Toby remembered ever hearing it before. 'I can't tell you how far we came to get here in time. Please don't let us fail now, after all this.'

The driver looked as if he thought he must be dreaming. He glanced away down the track, and Toby saw that his glasses were all steamed up. He gave a heavy sigh.

'All right then, young fellow, on you get. But keep your head down if my boss sees you, that's all I ask. And never tell anyone I did this. All right, I've a depot to get to.'

Toby felt uncle Nichol's hand gripping his own.

'Don't fail now, and don't be afraid.'

He caught one last glimpse of his uncle's face and he was in the goods train as it roared back into life. He glanced behind him and waved, but uncle Nichol had already disappeared. And all of a sudden Toby thought of Malice, Tweedledum and Tweedledee, the goats, Mrs MacPherson – everything and everybody he'd encountered in the last days at Alumbria – they were swept away in a single moment and he was going back to Edinburgh.

It was such a strange feeling – now on that goods train he wasn't at all sure that anything was real. Uncle Nichol's world felt like a dream and Edinburgh was so far away in his mind it was hard to believe it was really there.

'Fancy some cocoa?'

The driver's shout made him jump, he was so far away in his own thoughts. But he nodded all the same.

'All right, help yourself. You'll find a thermos behind you there. Should be a clean cup. You won't taste better if you walked a thousand miles to find it. My old mum's.' Toby poured himself a cupful and thought of his own mum. How long was it since she'd made him cocoa? She used to make it for him when he couldn't sleep, when he tossed and turned and began to whimper so she padded into his bedroom with sweet, warm cocoa. She used to turn his pillow over and give it what she called 'the magic touch.' He always did sleep after that and he always believed that the magic touch was real. He sipped the cocoa and felt the warmth burrowing right down to his toes. He shivered. His mum was the real thing he had to believe in now. Nothing else mattered much else apart from her. He remembered his uncle's last words to him – *don't fail now, and don't be afraid.* Often he thought he was probably the most frightened person in the whole world, but now he wasn't so sure. Maybe everyone really felt the same inside; it was just that some people were better at hiding it. Grown-ups were usually better at it, but he'd never seen uncle Nichol afraid and never in all his wildest dreams would he have imagined before that his mad, bold uncle might ever suffer real fear. He would never have believed it. Now he knew better. He knew that the world was a much stranger place than he'd thought before.

'Why the hurry into Edinburgh then?' Again the driver's loud voice almost made him leap through the roof of the train.

'Not often I see a young boy and an old fellow waving at me like windmills at five in the morning.'

'There's someone I have to see,' Toby said. He felt a lump grow in his throat as he spoke the words, and he hoped and he hoped that the train driver wouldn't ask him any more because he couldn't have answered.

But the driver didn't ask any more. He just nodded. Maybe he did understand in his own way; maybe he knew he should leave Toby's answer at that. Toby stood beside him, looking out into the darkness ahead of them. The lights of the train were sweeping away the darkness as they sped towards Edinburgh. It was a bit like being in a snowplough, clearing away darkness from the railway lines and piling it in strange black loads into the fields and woods alongside them. For just a bit those were the only things Toby thought about – the darkness that was like snow, the lights of the train, and the warm cocoa that burned sweetly in his tummy.

'You can catch forty winks if you like,' the driver said to him. 'You look white as a sheet, you do, and it's still another hour to Edinburgh. I'll be sure to waken you once we get there. I can't take you all the way to my depot or the boss'll fry me for breakfast, but I'll stop at a siding and let you off safe and sound.'

Toby nodded. They seemed like the best words he'd heard in a long time. He found himself a seat in the shadows of the driver's van and fell down into it. He was still thinking about all the things that were used to make cocoa when he fell fast asleep. He dreamed that he was offered all the cocoa in the world for just one grain of his star dust. A dark voice was asking him over and over again but he kept shaking his head – he mustn't give in. . . .

'Here, young 'un! Wakey, wakey then, or my life won't be worth living when the boss catches you here!'

Toby rubbed his eyes and sat up. Even though he hadn't slept properly for so long he felt quite alert right away. The goods train wasn't making much noise, just a clanking as it rolled over certain sleepers. The quiet was eerie. Everything in the whole world seemed grey – the buildings, the skies, the fences, the trees, the grass. Toby realised at that moment just how very much he didn't want to go back to the city. He felt it somewhere in the bottom of his tummy – it was like eating something wrong that wouldn't go away. Then the driver pointed.

'Look! There's a fox! See it, running down the side of that

drive? They use the railway lines, you know. They use them like we use roads. Come in and out from the country.'

Toby watched the fox, saw it turning its head to watch the train. Even it was grey, apart from the jet-black tip of its tail. But then he saw something else, a tall tower over behind a bridge, and he recognised it.

'That's where I'm going! Over there!' he exclaimed.

The driver glanced at him. 'The hospital? Is that where you're heading in such a hurry? All right, just another couple of minutes to the siding and you promise not to tell a single soul I brought you here.'

The train slowed and squealed to a complete standstill. Toby gave his word. The driver stuck out his hand to shake Toby's. It was big and soft; his fingers were like sausages. But somehow Toby felt he really meant that handshake. It was full of warmth and kindliness and well-wishing.

'Take care, son,' he said gently.

'Thank you,' Toby said.

He jumped from the footplate and onto the concrete of the siding. In just a few steps he'd chased up the embankment to a path. He glanced back down and saw the engine driver still there, making sure he was all right. Toby smiled and waved. He could feel the star dust next to his heart. There wasn't a soul about. It was as if everybody had gone to look at something and left the city fast asleep. Toby thought it looked almost beautiful. All the places he knew so well were carved out of mist – the Castle and Arthur's Seat and the Scott Monument – they seemed made out of mist. For a second he had to stop and look at them, and listen to this amazing silence on the morning of the 1st of March.

A ridiculous thought went through his head. Maybe the visit to the Little Moon had changed everything, had stopped time completely. But then how would the train have passed them at the station. . . ? Toby blinked the thought away. Edinburgh would wake up soon enough just as it always did.

He looked back down the embankment and saw that the goods train had vanished now – all he could hear was the last fading noise of it. Toby knew he had to run; he had to run as never before in his life. He took a deep breath and he looked at the hospital ahead of him in the mist, and he ran.

Nothing was going to stand between him and Ward 8 any longer. This was why he'd come back and he could hardly bear to waste even these few minutes running now. All that mattered was getting there. He didn't look at his feet; he kept the windows of the hospital in his sights and he ran. That was the window he had seen many times in his mind when he'd been at Alumbria and in the rocket and on the Little Moon. He ran as straight as he could and when he got to the steps he just bent forwards, his hands on his knees, gasping for breath as if his chest would burst.

Once he'd recovered he started thinking. He lifted his head and looked right at a red-brick clock tower rising into the sky. Ten to seven. The first black taxi hummed round a corner, looking for all the world like a big shiny beetle. Soon the streets would be a stream of buses and cars and lorries as the rush hour began. But not yet. He had to think clearly now. He glanced behind him at the main doors. Wouldn't it be better to find a side entrance, a way in that would hide him? He had to reach his mum alone; if a nurse came with him he would never be able to explain about the star dust, or give her some. But if he was caught trying to get in somewhere else it might be even worse. . .

Toby didn't know what on earth he should do. He heard his heart pounding in his chest; he looked at the glass doors of the entrance and wondered and wondered. It was almost seven o'clock. They would be getting breakfast ready. If he didn't make a move now his chance would be lost. He heard uncle Nichol's words echoing in his ears: *You've faced the lions*. This was the last lot he had to face and there was no way out.

At that moment he heard the slamming of a side door. A white van had stopped at the bottom of the steps, its engine still purring.

'Be all right for a minute, Bert,' one man was shouting to the other as they both struggled up the steps with heavy boxes.

Toby bit his lip. As they passed him he got up, shadowed them as they whistled into the building and turned to ask the staff at the reception desk where they should leave their delivery. Toby half-ran in the other direction, willing them not to see him. He came to some stairs and started his way up; behind him he could still hear the two men laughing as they chatted to the staff in the office.

On the next landing he had to flatten himself against a wall. Three nurses had just come into the corridor from the far end; they were laughing and chatting and paying no attention to anything else. He slid into a side room he realised must be a cupboard. It was almost pitch dark and it smelled strongly of some medicine or other – a smell that reminded him of when he was very young and had to take cough mixture he hated. The three voices came closer, stopped not that far away.

'You going abroad for Easter, Julie? I might have known,

you're always going to exotic places! Me? Chance would be a fine thing! Can't afford it. The furthest I'll be going's my bed. Listen, d'you want me to find out about those drops for Mrs Arnold? Off you go and get your breakfast, Julie. Catch you later.'

Toby held his breath. If one of them was to come in now that would be it. He'd be in the most dreadful trouble. One of the nurses walked right past where he was hiding; he heard the other two going off down another corridor.

He put his head round the door; the coast was clear. But which way should he go? It was as difficult to know as when he stood outside, wondering which the safest way to come in would be. Everywhere seemed a road into danger. Then he caught sight of a sign for a lift, a service lift. Could he risk it? He'd a long way to go to reach Ward 8. There was almost no hope of getting there without being found. He glanced both ways and then flickered as quiet as a ghost across the corridor and shut the doors of the lift. As long as no-one else stopped it on the way up! He had to hope – that was all he could do. It was still early in the morning and the hospital seemed half asleep. This was the best chance he was going to get and he had to take it. He pushed the button to begin the journey up and the lift hummed and rattled as it rose through the floors. Every second that passed seemed to Toby like an eternity. He willed the lift to keep going, to make it safely. With a loud boom it came to a standstill. He was on the right floor now. All that remained was to find his mother. He had to work out where he was as quickly as he could. He opened the doors of the lift, peered cautiously out. The nurse's station was close by; it sounded as if two of them were there. His heart sank.

He had to get past them to reach the ward, to find his mother. He listened.

'So you're going to be staying in that one, are you, Sal?'

'Reckon so, I'm not a hundred per cent sure. . . You see that red door in the bottom right hand of the picture . . .'

Toby took his chance. They must be looking at something together on the counter. If he could be as quick and quiet as possible. . . He got down on all fours and started along the floor for all the world like a puppy. He got to the nurse's station and swept round it in a few seconds, his feet and hands hardly making a sound as they went.

The nurses were so busy with their talk they didn't hear a thing, nor did they catch sight of the strange dark shadow that flickered round the corner and was gone.

He dared look up. There was his mother's room. He was out of sight of the nurses. He got to his feet and soundlessly turned the handle. Two white faces looked at him in astonishment. Not just his mum – his dad was there too.

'Toby, what on earth are you doing here?' His dad started round the side of the bed towards him. His voice was filled with surprise, worry, annoyance and relief – all at the same time. Maybe it was now he had to be most brave of all. Maybe this was the real moment of courage.

His mum was sitting up in bed against a stack of pillows. Her face was white as the new-fallen snow he'd gone out to sledge in round Alumbria. He looked at her and the surprise had gone from her face. He glanced at the window behind her, the one he'd imagined so often in his mind at Alumbria.

Suddenly he realised that the nurses might come at any moment, they might come and his one chance would be lost for ever. Fear gripped him more than anything else, and fear made him pull himself together and act.

'Uncle Nichol and I. . . we found something for you, mum. That's why I'm here. We had to go a long way to get it, but. . . '

He began tugging at the tiny bag of star dust in his inside pocket. He could hear the nurses coming along Ward 8.

'What on earth are you talking about?' his dad said, pulling him round. 'And where's uncle Nichol? He should be with you!'

Toby looked at his mum and swallowed hard as he freed the bag.

'Leave him, John. Let him explain,' she said softly.

'I'll tell you the whole story, as soon as there's a chance,' he breathed. 'But this is what really matters.'

He began pouring some of the precious crystals from the Little Moon into the glass on the cabinet beside his mother's bed.

'Star dust,' he whispered.

He handed the glass to his mother.

'Drink some. It's perfectly safe. Promise.'

She looked at him for a second, her eyes wide, and then she took just a sip. She looked round, bewildered. The nurses were talking loudly next door; they would be there any minute. Then his mother took another sip, and another. She looked at Toby clearly, her eyes open and alert. His dad sat down at the bottom of the bed, watching her, not knowing what to say. Toby realised he couldn't remember the last time he'd seen his mother looking well, and he felt something like an apple in his throat.

'I feel better,' she murmured, as though that was something

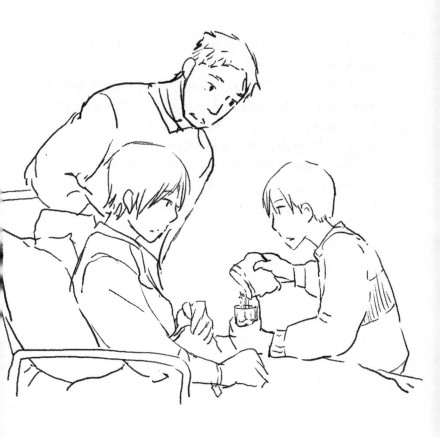

impossible. She smiled and he was almost sure there was colour in her cheeks.

She looked at Toby's dad and reached out for his hand; she put down the glass and caught Toby's hand too.

'Your dad's here because he didn't find a house,' she said. 'Isn't that right, John?'

He nodded and looked at Toby.

'She's absolutely right. And I looked at eight houses.'

Suddenly she leaned forwards, gripped their hands more tightly.

'What about moving to Alumbria? To uncle Nichol's? Once I'm better?'

'I'm not doing the hoovering, that's for sure!' said Toby's dad, and how the three of them laughed. Toby was so happy he wanted to cry. He was bursting with happiness, for with every passing second his mum looked better.

She looked at him and her eyes sparkled.

'When you were born,' she said, 'on February the 29th, I knew you would be special. There was a full moon. I was looking out and a shadow passed over the moon, just before you were born.'

He smiled and nodded. He understood. Now he understood.